"Am I Making

Shallie closed her ey[...]
dissolving into a mist[...]

"For making love with me?" Mac asked.

"For thinking...for wanting..." She hesitated.

"For wanting something more for yourself?" he
finished for her.

When she nodded, he cupped her jaw, gently
turned her head so she had to look at him.

"Where's the harm, Shallie? We're both
unattached, healthy adults who care deeply about
each other. I trust you. You trust me. What could
possibly be wrong with making each other feel
good?"

"Nothing," she whispered. "Nothing at all."

"So we won't be sorry in the morning?"

"I've been sorry for a lot of things in my life.
I can't imagine that spending a night with you
would be one of them...."

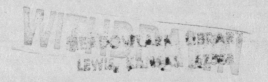

Dear Reader,

Things are heating up in our family dynasty series, THE ELLIOTTS, with *Heiress Beware* by Charlene Sands. Seems the rich girl has gotten herself into a load of trouble and has ended up in the arms of a sexy Montana stranger. (Well...there are worse things that could happen.)

We've got miniseries galore this month, as well. There's the third book in Maureen Child's wonderful SUMMER OF SECRETS series, *Satisfying Lonergan's Honor,* in which the hero learns a startling fifteen-year-old secret. And our high-society continuity series, SECRET LIVES OF SOCIETY WIVES, features *The Soon-To-Be-Disinherited Wife* by Jennifer Greene. Also, Emilie Rose launches a brand-new trilogy about three socialites who use their trust funds to purchase bachelors at a charity auction. TRUST FUND AFFAIRS gets kicked off right with *Paying the Playboy's Price.*

June also brings us the second title in our RICH AND RECLUSIVE series, which focuses on wealthy, mysterious men. *Forced to the Altar,* Susan Crosby's tale of a woman at the mercy of a...yes...wealthy, mysterious man, will leave you breathless. And rounding out the month is Cindy Gerard's emotional tale of a pregnant heroine who finds a knight in shining armor with *A Convenient Proposition.*

So start your summer off right with all the delectable reads from Silhouette Desire.

Happy reading!

Melissa Jeglinski

Melissa Jeglinski
Senior Editor
Silhouette Books

Please address questions and book requests to:
Silhouette Reader Service
U.S.: 3010 Walden Ave., P.O. Box 1325, Buffalo, NY 14269
Canadian: P.O. Box 609, Fort Erie, Ont. L2A 5X3

CINDY GERARD

A Convenient
Proposition

Published by Silhouette Books

America's Publisher of Contemporary Romance

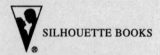

SILHOUETTE BOOKS

ISBN 0-373-76734-X

A CONVENIENT PROPOSITION

Copyright © 2006 by Cindy Gerard

Visit Silhouette Books at www.eHarlequin.com

Printed in U.S.A.

Books by Cindy Gerard

Silhouette Desire

The Cowboy Takes a Lady #957
Lucas: The Loner #975
*The Bride Wore Blue #1012
*A Bride for Abel Greene #1052
*A Bride for Crimson Falls #1076
†The Outlaw's Wife #1175
†Marriage, Outlaw Style #1185
†The Outlaw Jesse James #1198
Lone Star Prince #1256
In His Loving Arms #1293
Lone Star Knight #1353
The Bridal Arrangement #1392

The Secret Baby Bond #1460
Taming the Outlaw #1465
*The Librarian's Passionate
  Knight* #1525
Tempting the Tycoon #1539
Breathless for the Bachelor #1564
Storm of Seduction #1583
*Between Midnight and
  Morning* #1630
Black-Tie Seduction #1665
A Convenient Proposition #1734

*Northern Lights Brides
†Outlaw Hearts

Silhouette Books

Family Secrets
The Bluewater Affair

CINDY GERARD

Since her first release in 1991 hit the National #1 slot on the Waldenbooks bestseller list, Cindy Gerard has repeatedly made appearances on several bestseller lists, including *USA TODAY*.

With numerous industry awards to her credit—among them the Romance Writers of America's RITA® Award and the National Reader's Choice Award—this former Golden Heart finalist and repeat *Romantic Times BOOKclub* nominee is the real deal. As one book reviewer put it, "Cindy Gerard provides everything romance readers want in a love story—passion, gut-wrenching emotion, intriguing characters and a captivating plot. This storyteller extraordinaire delivers all of this and more!"

Cindy and her husband, Tom, live in the Midwest on a minifarm with quarter horses, cats and two very spoiled dogs. When she's not writing, she enjoys reading, traveling and spending time at their cabin in northern Minnesota unwinding with family and friends. Cindy loves to hear from her readers and invites you to visit her Web site at www.cindygerard.com.

This book is dedicated to readers everywhere.
As a writer, I am so grateful for your passion and
enthusiasm and support of what I do.

One

A winter sky hung heavy over the Shadow range, spitting dime-size snowflakes like a white blanket shedding lint. As the rattletrap of a pickup slowly approached Sundown, Montana, Shallie Malone stared through the passenger side windshield, wishing she could shake the notion that maybe this snowstorm was an omen. Maybe coming back to Sundown was a huge mistake.

Imagine that. Her making another mistake. So what else was new?

She expelled a weary sigh as the old truck bounced along the snow-packed road. She'd made a lot of mistakes in her twenty-seven years. She hadn't wanted her return to Sundown to be one of them, though. She'd wanted it to be—well, she'd wanted it to feel like home again, not like another misstep on the very rocky road of life.

Face it, she thought, as a jagged line of mountain peaks disappeared behind a heavy clot of clouds; mistake or not, it wasn't like she'd really had many other choices.

She focused on the forest beyond the windshield as the wipers shoved wet flakes off the glass. The pine boughs bent like old shoulders under the weight of winter. She, too, felt very old today. And weighted down. Mr. Coleman, the elderly rancher who she vaguely remembered had been kind enough to give her a lift from the bus station in Bozeman. He had the heater going full blast. Even so, Shallie shivered beneath her lightweight jacket. And tried to ignore the queasy feeling in the pit of her stomach—the feeling that suggested the old adage might be true: You can't go home again.

A name on a mailbox at the end of what she knew was a long curving lane leading deep into the forest and halfway up the mountain caught her eye as they drove by.

She cranked her head around to catch another glimpse of black lettering partly covered with snow. "Did that say Brett McDonald?"

"Hum? Oh, yeah." Concentrating on keeping the truck from slipping off the slick road, Bob Coleman squinted through his bifocals after a cursory glance at his rearview mirror. "The boy bought the old Fremont place about the same time he bought the Dusk to Dawn."

Whoa. Mac? Her childhood buddy, Brett "Mac" McDonald, now owned the Fremont cabin? And she couldn't believe what else Bob Coleman had just said. "The Haskins sold the Dusk to Dawn?"

"Beats all, don't it?" Bob grimaced beneath the brim of a worn gray Stetson. "Never thought I'd see the day when Nadine and Chet would hang it up, but I guess they got a hankering to do some traveling and Mac had the cash to make it happen."

The Dusk to Dawn was Sundown, Montana's, local watering hole for the community and the ranchers surrounding town. It was bar, restaurant, coffee shop and minimart all wrapped up in one well-used, well-loved establishment. If someone got married, the reception was held at the Dusk to Dawn. If someone died, it was where the family had the wake. Birthday parties, graduations and regular Saturday-night party-hardy crowds had gathered under the green tin roof for as long as Sundown had been Sundown. And for as long as Shallie had known Sundown, the Haskins had run the Dusk to Dawn.

Finding out that they were no longer there—a major change to something so stable—made her a little sad. She'd been a long time coming home. She hadn't wanted to see changes. She'd wanted everything to be the same as when she'd left. There was security in the status quo, and that's what she needed most right now.

Foolish, yeah. But it had been comforting to think that in a world in constant evolution, Sundown with its slow pace and plain, honest folk would always remain pretty much what it had been.

"Seems Mac made quite a business for himself in Bozeman," Bob added, oblivious to Shallie's melancholy thoughts. "Got himself a fancy I-*tal*-ian restaurant folks flock to from all over. I've even taken the missus there a time or two when we could get a reservation. Word is he decided he'd just as well branch out a bit and bring some business back home."

Mac was a hometown boy. Thinking of him running, as Bob Coleman put it, a fancy Italian restaurant made Shallie grin.

Wild. Lord, had that boy been wild. Not mean wild. Devilish, fun-loving wild. Whatever mischief he and John Tyler couldn't think of to stir up when they were kids wasn't worth talking about. More often than not, she'd been in on making some of that trouble with them.

Shallie sobered. *Trouble.* Imagine that. Didn't take long to come back around to the point that she was in trouble again.

She placed a hand protectively over her flat tummy and the budding new life sleeping there. Assured herself that coming back was a good thing. The right thing. And when the truck rounded the ridge and the tiny hamlet of Sundown came into view, the little shiver of unease shifted to anticipation and told her, yes. Yes, this *was* right.

How many times had she driven this road and seen Sundown from this vantage point, nestled in the valley like a multicolored and well-worn skirt at the base of the Shadow range? That skirt was now blanketed in white. Chimney smoke spiraled up in wispy drifts, like steam rising from a bubbling kettle. How many times had she taken this simple beauty for granted?

Way too many.

Well, she wouldn't make that particular mistake again.

She was almost home. At least she was as close to home as she'd ever been. She might be coming back with her head held low in shame, but she wouldn't let her decision to return turn into another mistake. More to the point, she wasn't going to make the same mistakes her own mother had made.

Okay, she amended, absently touching her tummy again. She wasn't going to make *all* of the same mistakes. Joyce Malone had let down everyone who'd ever counted on her—including, Shallie figured, herself.

They'd no sooner rounded a switchback on a steep downhill grade when a sleek black pickup came roaring up the road and snapped her out of her thoughts. The club cab fishtailed on the slick skiff of new snow glazing the road's surface and headed straight toward them.

"Tarnation," Bob muttered.

He jerked the steering wheel hard right to avoid getting clipped by the big truck. "Hang on," he said, his jaw tight, his hands white on the wheel as he slammed on the brakes.

When Shallie saw the size of the tree directly ahead of them, she braced a hand against the dash and clamped her jaw together to keep from screaming.

Not that it worked. The sound that came out of her mouth was just this side of ear splitting. And the pain that knifed through her wrist when the truck crashed to a stop in a drift made her physically ill.

Swearing under his breath, Brett McDonald brought his truck to a skidding stop on the shoulder of the road. Damn. He hadn't seen that patch of ice. But he had seen Bob Coleman's pickup—and just in the nick of time. He'd risked rolling his truck to miss it. Thank God he *had* missed it—just barely.

Jamming the gearshift into park, he set the emergency brake and shoved open the door. Heart hammering like a piston, he jumped to the ground. Engine exhaust rose in white clouds as he sprinted toward Bob's truck, scared to death the old man had gotten hurt when he'd swerved to miss him.

The good news: the old Ford had stopped in a snowbank just short of a head-on with a huge white pine. Not a scratch on it. The bad news: the truck was sitting sideways on the narrow road; the front bumper buried deep into the drift the plow had left along the shoulder.

"You okay, Bob?" Mac yelled through the rancher's closed window.

"Yeah, I believe I'm of a piece." Bob turned his head toward the passenger seat. "What about you, Shallie? You okay over there?"

Shallie? Mac had only ever known one Shallie—but this couldn't be *his* Shallie.

He ducked his head so he could see across the cab. My God. His heart hit him a couple of good ones as old memories and old feelings tussled with the shock of seeing her.

Shallie. His Shallie Malone. He hadn't seen her since high school, when she'd lit out of Sundown like her tail was on fire. But he'd recognize those big brown eyes and that tangle of short brown curls anywhere.

And he'd recognize the mad scramble of his heartbeat and the catch in his breath as the reaction he'd always had around this woman. Okay. She'd been a girl last time he'd seen her. That hadn't made his feelings for her any less real. She didn't know it—he'd been too proud to ever spill his guts about how he felt about her—but Shallie Malone had been the one. The one that got away.

He scrambled around to the passenger side, waded through the knee-deep snow and jerked the door open with a grin on his face. Shallie was back—and unless she was married, engaged or otherwise taken, she wasn't getting away this time.

"Shallie! Darlin'. If you aren't a sight for sore eyes."

She'd been one fine-looking girl. She was beyond fine as a woman. His grin faded, though, when he searched her face and saw the unmistakable strain of pain in her eyes.

"Oh, damn." His heart sank as concern tangled with self-disgust. "You're hurt."

She shot him a valiant smile. "Leave it to you, McDonald. I travel almost two thousand miles without a scratch, then I'm one mile from home and you manage to break my wrist."

Two

"Okay, worrywart, you can wipe that death-door look off your face," Shallie assured Mac as she walked out of the emergency room three hours later. "I'm fine. It's hardly more than a sprain."

Mac's breath of relief when he finally saw her was tinged with the antiseptic scent of hospital. He rose from the hard, waiting-room chair and hurried toward her. Her brown eyes looked up at him from a face that was pale and weary. Dark smudges of fatigue painted violet bruises beneath her eyes.

Her left arm was supported by a sling. Inside the sling he could see what looked like a cast. *Sonofabitch.* He'd done this to her. "If it's just a sprain, why did they put it in a cast?"

She shrugged, as if the cast was of little importance.

"Okay," she finally conceded when he gave her a hard look. "So maybe it's a hairline fracture."

"Then it's *broken*," he pointed out with a sinking sensation in his gut as she tried, again, to minimize the damage. *Damn.* He'd broken her wrist.

Though pain pinched tight lines around the corners of her mouth, she still worked up a smile for him. "Well, if you're going to do something, just as well do it right."

"Damn, darlin'." He slung an arm over her shoulders when what he wanted to do was fold her into his arms and absorb all of her pain. Instead, feeling protective and responsible, and like a first-class ass, he pressed a kiss to the top of her head. "I am *so* sorry."

"Stop." She gave him a squeeze with her good arm, then pushed away from him. "I'm fine. Quit beating yourself up."

He needed more than a beating. He needed to be drawn and quartered for putting her in this fix. Once he'd bundled her into his truck, then made certain Bob Coleman and his pickup were okay and back on the road, he'd headed straight for Bozeman and the hospital.

She'd sputtered and tried to minimize the damage all the way. "I just *came* from Bozeman. And I don't need to see a doctor. I was joking about it being broken, for Pete's sake. It's just banged up a little."

It was just banged up a *lot.* Mac had suspected as much from the way she so very carefully cradled it against her ribs. He'd have given anything not to be right.

"They give you anything for the pain?" He snagged her jacket from the chair where he'd been holding on to it for her.

"I'll do fine with some Tylenol."

"You need something a helluva lot stronger than that," he insisted, helping her slip her good arm into the right sleeve. Carefully settling the jacket over her shoulders, he fought the urge to leave his hands there and pull her back against him. "What's the matter with that doctor?"

"I said no to a prescription, okay?" She glanced at him over her shoulder, then looked away, like there was more she had been about to tell him but changed her mind at the last second.

She'd said no to a lot of things since he'd found her in Bob's truck, Mac suddenly realized. Like medical care for starters. Mac had finally figured out why when they'd checked in at the E.R. desk. She didn't have health insurance.

The lightbulb finally went on. Which was probably why she'd refused the pain medication, Einstein. Maybe she can't afford it.

"Look, short-stack," Mac turned away to snag his own jacket, reverting to his old nickname for her because of her love for pancakes, "I already told you, I'm picking up the tab for this. It's my fault. That makes it my bill. Besides, my vehicle insurance will cover it, so it's nothing out of my pocket. Now...let's reconsider that prescription, okay?"

But she was already heading out the door.

On an exasperated breath, Mac stomped after her.

"Same ol' hardhead," he muttered. That was one of the things he'd loved about her. She was stubborn and strong and a survivor, in spite of what she'd had to endure growing up. She'd been a damn stubborn girl. Stood to reason that she'd grown into a damn stubborn woman. A damn beautiful woman. A woman who had set the bar for all others, none of whom had measured up.

"Okay," he conceded, catching up with her as he cleared the revolving door. "We do it your way—for now. But if I hear so much as a whimper of pain or see that you're suffering, we're going to have us a little talk."

"Let's talk anyway," she suggested as they walked side by side toward his truck. "How the heck are you, McDonald?"

Mac cupped the elbow of her right arm—telling himself it was to steady her and not because he couldn't resist touching her—as they picked their way carefully across the snow-covered parking lot.

"Hungry, that's how I am," he said hoping she wouldn't notice how aware he was of her.

The snow had started falling like it was going to get serious again by the time they reached his truck. With his hand still on her elbow, he punched the keyless remote and opened the passenger door. "How about we talk over a nice hot meal?"

That was one way to keep her with him a little longer.

"Works for me," she said as he helped her step up onto the running board then ease into the seat. "As long as it's not Italian."

His face must have fallen because she laughed and, making a gun with the thumb and forefinger of her right hand, fired at him. "Gotcha."

He grinned as he buckled her in then walked around and slid behind the wheel. "Har, har. It would be nice to think that news of my restaurant has spread far and wide." Just like it would be nice to think that maybe she'd kept track of him during the past several years and that's why she knew about his restaurant. But that amounted to ego and wishful thinking drawing the conclusions.

"If it makes you feel good, then you go right ahead and think it."

What would make him feel good was if she was pressed up against him on this cold winter night, but that was just crazy. So he grinned his good-ol'-boy grin instead of suggesting she slide on over close. "What I'm thinking is that Bob Coleman, as usual, must have done a lot of talking."

"No one would argue with you on that one," she said with a smile that looked like it zapped all of her energy.

She was dead beat, Mac realized as he cranked up the heat and headed out of the lot. And still beautiful and still turning him on like a strobe light.

Shallie. He still couldn't believe it. What stroke of luck had prompted her to return to Sundown after— what? Nine? Ten years?

He'd find out soon enough. In the meantime he didn't really care what had brought her back into his life. Or why she'd left and he'd never heard from her again. He was just damn glad she was here. He'd never stopped thinking about her—which was just plain dumb since he'd probably only crossed her mind in passing now and again in the past several years.

But still, despite the fact that he was responsible for breaking her wrist, he was happy as hell that he'd *almost* run into her today.

* * *

"I have to stop." Shallie reluctantly pushed away her plate of tortellini carbonara. She was too full to eat another bite. "I don't want to, but I have to. Good Lord, Mac, this food is amazing."

"That would be *good* amazing, right?"

Mac's lively blue eyes danced in his familiar, handsome face that still bore shades of a summer tan. She'd forgotten how blue his eyes were. Montana-sky blue. Still smiling. Still teasing. Still the eyes of a friend.

It was so good to see him. Not that Shallie was willing to simply come out and say so. That wasn't the way things had ever worked between them. She'd known. Even as a girl she'd known that, with a little encouragement, Mac would have taken their relationship past friendship into something more.

And it had been tempting. But tempting as it had been—as tempting as it might be now—she hadn't needed a boyfriend back then. She'd needed a friend. Just like she needed one now. Bottom line, she could not afford to screw things up between them. She'd never forgive herself if she did.

Besides, it would have been easy to fall in love with Mac. Looking at him now, it would still be easy. Too easy. She didn't trust easy. *Easy* wasn't a word that had ever been a part of her life experience. Especially where men were concerned. And when it had started to look easier to let her teenage emotions take over and fall that little bit of distance in love with Brett McDonald, she'd left Sundown. Running scared away from her emotions. It would have ended badly, and bad was something she couldn't bear when it came to Mac. That's why she hadn't kept in touch. She'd had to make the break clean. Final.

"Yeah. That would be good amazing," she said in response to his fishing expedition, then fell back into the safe pattern of gentle ribbing they'd established as kids. "Some things never change, I see. You're still trolling for compliments."

"What can I say? I've got a big ego. It needs lots of stroking."

That was so not true. He *should* have an ego; it was amazing that he didn't. Mac had always been the cutest, the most athletic, the smartest, the most macho, most sought after guy in school. Not by her, of course, because she *had* been very careful to always treat him like a brother. But he'd never taken himself—or his looks—seriously.

Speaking of serious, aside from the circumstances that had prompted her return to Sundown, and aside from her broken wrist, it had finally started to feel like she *had* done the right thing in coming home again. And sitting here with Mac smiling at her across the table in a quiet corner in his restaurant, Spaghetti Western, was reason enough to have come back.

Mac was her friend. She was mature enough now to keep him in that niche. One of the best she'd ever had. He'd been one of the few constants, the few comforts in a childhood where she'd lived a far cry from Mr. Rogers's neighborhood. In this moment he felt as comfortable as a warm blanket on this cold, end-of-December night. And comfortable was the extent of the feelings she could afford to let herself have for him.

"Damn it's good to see you," Mac said, shaking his head as if he couldn't believe she was really here. "So what brings you back to Montana, doll face?"

Logical question. The double trip of her heart was not, however, a logical response. Good friend or not, she wasn't quite ready to come clean with that little tidbit of information. Equal measures of guilt and shame kept her from telling him about the baby. At least for now.

"Just had a yearning to see the mountains again in the winter," she said evasively.

She glanced away when his eyes said they didn't quite buy her explanation. He'd always known her a little too well. But he didn't press, and for that she was grateful.

"And to see *you,* of course," she added, realizing how true it was. She really had missed him. Missed her friend, and she felt real bad, suddenly, that she'd allowed them to lose contact over the years.

"I'm sorry I haven't been much for staying in touch."

He lifted a shoulder in a throwaway shrug but she sensed, more than saw, the hurt behind his reaction. "Goes both ways. I'm just as guilty. It's a guy thing," he added with a grin.

"So catch me up," she prompted, smiling across a table draped in a charming red-and-white-checkered cloth. A white tapered candle burned between them, the flame flickering, making shadows dance across a masculine face that had matured with amazing grace. "How are your folks? Are they still in Sundown?"

"Dad is." He hesitated then added, "Mom's in L.A. They divorced several years ago."

If he had said they'd moved to the moon, she couldn't

have been more shocked. Tom and Carol McDonald had seemed like the perfect couple. Loving, caring, fun. They'd been the perfect family. Perfect parents. The ones she'd always wished she'd had. "Oh, Mac. I'm sorry."

"Yeah." His jaw hardened. "Me, too."

She wanted to ask what had happened. But she saw an uncharacteristic bleakness in Mac's eyes and understood that he didn't want to talk about it. That it was very painful for him.

"So what's happened to the old gang in the last nine years?" she asked brightly, determined not to put a damper on the evening. "Where's J.T.? And Peg and the rest of the crew?"

She listened with interest as he ran down the list. Many of the kids they used to pal around with, it seemed, had left the little pond for bigger ones.

"Peg's still in Sundown, though," Mac said as he toyed absently with the stem of his wineglass.

Candlelight glinted off his dark hair, cast his hard jaw in shadow. Handsome, she thought as she watched his mobile mouth. Devastatingly handsome.

"Married with two kids. Settled in raising bucking stock with Cutter Reno and Lee and Ellie Savage."

Shallie blinked, shocked out of an unexpected fantasy of the press of his beautiful mouth to hers. *What was wrong with her?* "Reno? Peg married that outlaw? He was chasing silver belt buckles and women on the PRCA rodeo circuit last I knew."

"Yeah, well, he's about as far from an outlaw as Preacher Davis now. I'm told a good woman can do that for a bad man. Same goes for J.T."

"J.T.? John Tyler is married?" They had been the three musketeers—Shallie and J.T. and Mac.

Times do change. And don't think about his mouth. Or the thickness of his biceps beneath his shirt. Or the breadth of his hands, the length of his fingers…

"Yep. Just this fall," Mac continued, his smile returning while she forced herself to take a sip of water. "He did a stint in the military after college. Ended up in Afghanistan. Messed him up a little—not that anyone but me knew it. Anyway, he took a liking to the new vet, and the feeling was mutual."

She chanced a look at his face, then surprised them both by laughing when she realized what she saw in his expression. "And the idea that J.T. tied the knot makes you nervous as heck, doesn't it?"

J.T. and Mac had sworn they'd never get married. There may have even been a blood oath involved. Of course, they'd been eleven years old at the time. The three of them had been big on blood oaths back then.

"Me? Nah."

"Liar, liar," she teased in a sing-song voice.

He ignored her taunting. "J.T. can't help it if he went soft in the head. I'm made of sterner stuff. You won't catch me settled in with a ring in my nose—I mean, on my finger."

She shook her head. "You're awful."

His eyes twinkled. "Just calling it like I see it."

"Hmm. Or did word about that sour disposition of yours finally get out and any woman with half a brain knows enough to stay away from you?"

"Hey—" He affected a wounded look. "Some of my

favorite dates only have half a brain, so don't go bad-mouthing my taste."

Shallie rolled her eyes and hoped her curiosity about the women he dated didn't show.

"What about you, Shallie Mae? Where've you been? Whatcha been doing?"

Yeah, well, she'd known they'd get around to this sooner or later. She laid her napkin on the table by her plate. "Not much of a story there."

"Somehow I find that hard to believe."

"Believe it," she assured him, feeling more than self-conscious about her lackluster career. "School and work pretty much tell the tale. It took me eight years to get my degree."

That was because she'd had to work to pay her way through college, and sometimes she'd have to drop classes altogether to stay on top of the frills like food and rent and electricity.

"But now I are a teacher," she said, adapting a goofy grin to go with her goofy grammar. Both made him smile.

He leaned back in his chair, considered her, then nodded. "A teacher. That's cool, Shall. Really cool."

"Yeah," she said reacting to his warm smile with one of her own, remembering why he had always been so special to her. He was proud of her. He always had been. Even when she hadn't been able to muster up a shred of self-pride. "It is cool. Kindergarten."

"So, you're on winter break?"

She *would* have been on winter break if she hadn't been asked to let go of her contract when the school board in the small town in southeast Georgia had found out about her pregnancy. Unwed kindergarten teachers, it seemed, did not make the popularity list in small town, rural South. She knew she could have fought it and won. The truth was, she hadn't had any fight left in her. And she'd wanted to get away from the mess she'd made.

"Yeah," she said, instead of leveling with him. "I'm on break."

Silence settled and with it another layer of guilt. Shallie had the feeling Mac saw right through her lie. If he did, he didn't quiz her on it, thankfully. He wouldn't be so proud of her now if he knew the whole truth.

"You sure you don't want some wine?" he asked instead. "I've got a nice red in the cooler."

She shook her head. "None for me. You go ahead, though."

He gave her another one of those considering looks, but let it drop. "That's okay. I've had enough. Besides, you have to be beat. And don't lie, I know your wrist has to hurt like hell."

She *was* tired. And her wrist *did* hurt. "It *has* been a long day," she admitted without acknowledging the pain. "I thought I'd be holed up in the Sundown Hotel tonight, but it's a little too late to head back now. So, kind sir, if you'll point me to a decent motel here in Bozeman, I'm ready to call it a day."

He snorted. "Yeah, like that's going to happen. You're not staying in any motel," he informed her as if that was the most ridiculous idea he'd ever heard. "You're staying at my place here in Bozeman."

She shook her head. "Mac—"

"No," he insisted, cutting her off. "I've got an extra bedroom, extra bath. Cripes, Shallie, it's the least I can do after banging up your wrist. And before you wind up for a fight, save what energy you've got left. This is not open for debate. You're staying with me. End of story."

She knew from experience that she was dealing with one stubborn Irishman. She should fight it a little harder, but the thought of not having to hassle with checking into a cold, generic motel room was just too appealing.

"And what will the woman in your life think about another woman staying over?" She hadn't planned on asking about his women. She hadn't planned on being this curious, either. And until he answered, she hadn't realized how relieved she would be with his response.

"There's no woman. So there's no problem."

Now there was a tidbit of information that she could happily dwell on if she let herself. She didn't let herself.

"Okay. Fine. I'll stay. Add *bully* to *insufferable*," she groused through a smile that acknowledged she knew she'd met up with a brick wall and was actually grateful.

"Don't forget *incredible cook.*"

"And then some." Shallie stood when Mac did. "I'm not going to be able to eat for a week."

"So I shouldn't have the kitchen box up some tiramisu for a late night snack?"

"Tiramisu?" Oh my God. Tiramisu. Sweet. Chocolate. Heaven help her.

But she couldn't. Then her stomach growled.

He chuckled. "Thought that might perk you up. Still

got the same ol' sweet tooth, huh? Be right back." With a nod toward the front door, he pointed her to a waiting area and headed for the kitchen.

Shallie strolled over to the welcoming bench and sat, aware that she was smiling. Interesting. Despite her throbbing wrist, despite the fact that she had no idea what she was going to do for money now that she'd been given doctor's orders not to work for several weeks, she was smiling.

She shook her head at her own lack of concern about the direness of her circumstances. Then she cut herself a little slack. There'd be time enough to worry about money tomorrow. Tonight she was in the company of a special man, a good friend; she was warm, and her tummy was full.

And then there was the prospect of the tiramisu.

Just the tiramisu, she reminded herself when the delicious sight of Mac strolling toward her set a few hormones zinging in a very dangerous direction.

"Whoa," Shallie said as Mac rounded the last turn on a street on the outskirts of Bozeman and she got a look at his house. "The restaurant business must be *very* good."

Mac grinned as he punched the remote on his garage door opener, pulled into his drive and eased his new truck inside the triple-car garage. Yeah. The restaurant business was damn good. He'd just moved into the house he'd had built to his own specifications last month.

"Who knew that a love of spaghetti, a beer major and

a business minor could translate into the American dream."

He killed the motor, jumped down out of the truck and pocketed his keys, thinking it was a damn good thing he finally had a chance to put a little distance between them. Riding in the dark truck with soft music playing on his CD changer and nothing but dim dash lights and streetlights illuminating the night had made it a little too intimate. He'd clamped both hands on the wheel, finding himself resisting the urge to reach out and cover her hand with his a little too often.

What would she think if he had, he wondered. What would she think if he'd just covered her slim thigh with his hand, squeezed gently and said, "I've missed you, Shall. I've missed you, and this time I'm not letting you go."

She'd have slapped him up alongside the head, that's what she'd have done, he thought as he walked around to the other side of the truck. And he'd have deserved it.

She was tired. She was hurting. And if he knew his Shallie, there was something else working behind those intelligent eyes of hers. Something big. Something that bothered. Something—other than him—that had brought her back to Sundown.

All in good time, McDonald, he thought as he opened her passenger door. She'd tell him what was bothering her all in good time.

"It's stuck," she said, trying to work the seat belt latch one-handed under the stark, bright light in his three-car garage.

"Here. I'll get you out of there." He reached across her

lap and gave the buckle a try. And met with resistance. Not to mention the solid heat of woman beneath her thin jacket.

This could be trouble.

And it was.

"Damn. It *is* stuck. Hold on."

He climbed up on the running board and leaned across her so he could get a better angle—and ended up pressed against more of her with more of him. And the front seat of his big club-cab truck suddenly shrank to roughly the size of a soup bowl.

"Ah…" He fumbled with the latch and made it worse. "Oh. Here's the problem. It's your jacket. It's caught in the latch."

And he was caught up in lust. She was so soft and full against his arm. Her skin so pale and flawless.

Because she's exhausted, jackass. For God's sake, get a grip.

"Just get me a blanket and a pillow," she said dropping her head back against the leather seat and closing her eyes. "I'll be fine right here for the night."

She looked so tired right then that Mac figured she was halfway serious. And he had to do something to jar himself out of his sexual haze.

"Okay. Have a little faith, will ya? I'm not the sharpest tack in the drawer but I'm smarter than this seat belt and I don't care how many people say otherwise."

That pried a weary smile out of her. She'd always had such a pretty smile. Sure hadn't changed. Pretty smile. Pretty eyes—cinnamon brown shot through with gold. And she smelled good, too.

His head was merely inches from hers. Their bodies

bumped as he worked to free the seat belt latch. Strike
that. Her breast, *specifically,* brushed against his arm,
specifically, while he worked away at the jammed
buckle.

She felt soft and full against him. But this was
Shallie, he reminded himself. The woman who had
never wanted to be anything more than his friend.

A memory flashed. He'd been thirteen and in the
process of discovering what all the fuss was about over
the opposite sex. He'd tried to kiss her one night and
cop a feel, randy little brat that he'd been then. Not that
she'd let him get by with it. His tongue had been sore
for a week where she'd bitten it. His thumb had been
swollen for much longer after she'd bent it back to his
wrist and beyond.

But he'd never gotten over the thrill of that first, tentative contact. That wild, gut-knotting kick he'd experi-
enced when he'd touched her breast through her sweater.

"Don't you ever pull that crap with me again,
McDonald," she'd warned and, trying not to whimper
in pain, he'd promised that her mouth had seen the last
of his tongue.

And that should have ended any "awareness" of
Shallie Malone as a sex object.

It should have, but it hadn't. And he'd never felt the
same thrill in a kiss since.

"Any luck?"

He'd been so wrapped up in getting a handle on his
physical awareness that her question startled him. So
did a sudden realization. If he moved his head, turned
toward her just so, their mouths would be in perfect

alignment. He'd be able to experience firsthand the scent and taste of the chocolate mint she'd tucked in her mouth after dinner. And to find out up close and personal if those lush, full lips were as soft as they looked. If they still tasted the same. Like wild sex and young love and the sweetest heat this side of the equator.

The urge to find out—the strength of it—blindsided him.

"Nope," he said, jerking his attention back to the latch and putting all he had in resisting that urge. "Not yet. But if I don't have you out by morning, we may be looking at a lifelong commitment."

He hoped his little joke came out *sounding* like a joke instead of the desperate bid to break the unsettling sexual tension that had suddenly shrunk the inside of the truck yet again—this time to the size of a soup *spoon*. Man. Between running SW and working on the Dusk to Dawn, he'd pretty much been out of circulation. All work and no play and all that, made Mac a horny boy.

If only. The truth was, it was her. Just her that put him in this state.

"Got it," he said when the buckle finally gave. He backed out of the truck, feeling way too much regret that the warmth of her breast no longer heated his arm and way too little relief that his sojourn into lust was suddenly over.

But it *was* over. Over. Done. Never happened.

This was Shallie. Short-stack. The woman who only wanted to be his buddy. She'd kick his sorry butt clear across Montana if she knew what he'd been thinking. At least she would tonight. It was too soon. And it was

too much for now. With a little time, though. A little
time and a little patient persuasion, maybe, just maybe
all these years of waiting will have been worth it.

And as he helped her down out of the cab, though,
and retrieved the box of tiramisu and her one piece of
luggage, all of a sudden it didn't seem like such a bright
idea to have her sleeping across the hall from his
bedroom. What if he couldn't control himself?

"Now you're just being stupid," he muttered under
his breath as he unlocked the door to the house and let
them into the kitchen.

He held the door open for her and stepped back so she
could go inside ahead of him. "Being stupid about what?"

Once he flicked on a light, he didn't have to figure
out a plausible answer. She got sidetracked when she
saw his kitchen.

"You have *got* to be kidding."

Her eyes were wide with surprise and admiration as
she took in his state-of-the-art kitchen with its gleaming
stainless steel restaurant-grade appliances, black granite
countertop and large, multipaned skylight that was currently laden with snow.

Mac tossed his keys on the counter and shrugged out
of his jacket. "It's not much, but it's home," he said then
added on a proud grin that he just couldn't dampen,
"and damn spectacular, huh?"

"In a *word*." She continued to inspect and admire as
he helped her carefully out of her jacket. "Little Brett
McDonald. My. My. You've come a long way."

"Got lucky," he said, shrugging off the compliment.
"Come on. I'll give you the fifty-cent tour, but let me

warn you right now, I just moved in a few weeks ago. I don't even know where all the light switches are yet. I think there might even be a room or two that I haven't found."

Turning on lights as he went, he led her down three marble-tiled steps to the great room. A flip of another switch and the fire flickered to life in the native stone fireplace dominating the south wall from the floor to the ceiling that was two stories high.

Beside the fireplace stood a holdover from the season. A very dry and ready-to-pitch fifteen-foot Christmas tree was losing needles like a white dog shedding hair on a black sweater.

"If I know you—and I think I do," she said, "that poor tree has probably been up since the first of the month."

What could he say. He'd always been like a kid about Christmas.

Brittle needles had fallen on a yellow pine floor that gleamed under the soft light. A multicolored area rug in muted tones of greens and blues and tan was soft underfoot in the seating area.

"Oh, Mac. This is all so lovely."

"Well that's a kick in the butt. It's *supposed* to be masculine," he pointed out, making a show of sounding insulted as she crossed the room to run her fingers across a polished mantel cut from a single slab of rose-beige granite.

"Lovely and *masculine*," she amended. "It's also you."

It was the nicest compliment she could have paid him. Yeah, he'd hired a decorator to help him but he'd dictated the colors—rich jade greens, slate blues and taupe. At least, that's what the decorator called it. He called it sand.

He'd chosen the textures, too—native stone for the fireplace, warm wood for the floor and supple leathers for the furniture. And the artwork reflected his feelings for the Bozeman area.

He'd purchased all the pieces from locals artists— colorful, vibrant oil paintings of the mountains on the walls, metal and stone sculptures on the tables and floor blended with gas-fired pottery pieces on the mantel and hearth.

"Oh, sweetie, I'm sorry," he said when he realized she was about to topple over from fatigue, "I was having one of those God-I-love-this-place moments. They tell me it will wear off when I get my first tax bill."

He held out a hand. "Come on. Let's get you settled in. We can catch up some more in the morning. Unless you've got to be someplace. Man—I didn't even think of that. Do you? Have to be someplace?"

She shook her head and besides the exhaustion and pain, he swore he saw a brief but palpable sadness fill her eyes before she looked away. "Nope. No place to be. Nothing specific to do. I'm sure you've got plenty on your plate, though, so don't think you have to enter- tain me tomorrow."

His heart did a dance at the news she was free for a while. "Entertain you? Honey, this is Bozeman. In the winter. You'll be entertaining me."

He met her halfway across the room and folded her carefully into his arms again. He couldn't help it. For all she knew, it was simply a fraternal hug. He was hugging his friend who he was simply glad to see after so many years and whose presence brought back memories of good times and cheap thrills—that unfortunately had jump-started his hormones into thinking they should be perking right up after an unseasonably long hiatus.

Well. There you go, he thought. There was part of the explanation for reacting to her so strongly. Seeing her made him feel like a kid again—and he'd always been a randy kid.

"Remember the time we—you and J.T. and I—took Jacque, the foreign-exchange student out cow tipping?" he asked, reining things back into perspective.

She wrapped her good arm around his waist as he walked her toward the guest bedroom. "We were so bad."

She was grinning when she glanced up at him and for more reasons he didn't want to analyze, he was happy to see her smiling. "To the bone," he agreed, and all felt right with his world again.

Three

The next morning Shallie lay flat on her back in Mac's big guest room bed and wondered if she dared to get up. It had been a week since she'd had a bout of morning sickness, but that didn't mean it was over.

To be on the safe side, she'd just lie here for a little while longer. Plus, it was as good an excuse as any to wallow in this huge bed with the smooth, expensive sheets and soft, down mattress topper.

Heaven. Mac's house was absolute heaven. This bed was cloud-nine quality. She'd been afraid that her wrist would keep her awake. Or that she'd be too wired to sleep when he'd shown her to the spacious guest bedroom done in rich earth colors with brick-red accents. She'd been wrong on both counts.

Even with thoughts of the big carry-out container of

tiramisu tucked neatly in his spotless refrigerator waiting for her, she hadn't been able to make herself leave the comfort and warmth of this bed for a little midnight snack. Once she'd given it an experimental pat to test its firmness and discovered the down mattress beneath a plush native print comforter, she'd taken care of her bathroom ritual, slathered on some lotion, tugged on her favorite sleep shirt and had sunk into decadent luxury. She'd propped her throbbing arm on an extra pillow, closed her eyes and that was all she wrote.

Now it was morning. And she really should get a move on. She glanced down at her arm. Lifted it experimentally—and gasped. Every raw nerve in her body seemed to congregate in her wrist and remind her that broken bones—even hairline fractures—hurt like the devil.

"So, Malone…now what?" she wondered aloud as the pain dulled to a throbbing ache. She had virtually no use of her arm, so what was she going to do to support herself? Teaching was out of the question for the moment. Even though she hadn't anticipated finding a vacancy midterm, she'd hoped to find some substitute teaching work in the area. Maybe supplement her income waiting tables somewhere until she found a full-time position. She'd done plenty of waitressing when she'd worked her way through college. Sure, she had a little savings to tide her over and she had one more paycheck coming. Neither would last long, not with student loan payments and basic living expenses to cover.

Thankfully, a soft tap on the door diverted her attention from her financial dilemma.

"Hey, short-stack. You awake in there?"

Mac.

How could she not smile?

"Awake. But barely." She scooted up a little, flinching when her wrist protested.

"Are you decent?"

She propped one of the extra pillows behind her back. "I have *always* been decent. *Your* respectability, on the other hand, has always been questionable."

The door cracked open, and Mac, with a gorgeous smile, popped into the room. He was dressed in a plaid flannel shirt and tight, worn jeans, and if he'd been any man but Mac, she'd have thought, wow, I could get used to starting my mornings this way. He was gorgeous.

"Not nice to tick off the cook—especially when he's bearing breakfast in bed."

"Oh, my gosh. You shouldn't have done that. I'm already imposing. I don't want you cooking for me."

"Hel-lo. Cooking is what I do, remember?" He walked over to the bed carrying a tray laden with juice and coffee and pancakes that smelled like heaven—for about five seconds.

Oh, Lord.

Shallie threw back the covers, jumped out of bed and ran for the bathroom. Where she promptly got sick as a dog.

"Was it something I cooked?" Mac asked in a really feeble attempt at humor, hoping to undercut his concern.

"Oh, please. Go away. This is gross. I don't want you to have to deal with this."

And what are you dealing with, sweet friend of mine, Mac wondered, but didn't ask.

"Comes with the deluxe package at McDonald Inn." He wet a washcloth for her. "Clean sheets. Breakfast in bed. Nursing skills. It's printed on the door along with the rates. You must have missed it."

Poor baby. She looked so miserable. He squatted down on his haunches beside his little short-stack, a comforting hand gently rubbing her back as she hunched over the toilet bowl.

He would like to ignore the conclusions he'd started to draw. He'd like to think she was dealing was a case of nerves or the flu. If he was right about what he suspected, however, he wondered how long it was going to take her to come clean.

Hell. Maybe he was jumping recklessly to conclusions. He hoped so. He hoped to hell he was wrong about what he was thinking. Because if he was right, there was a serious chance that he was going to get good and pissed off before this day was over. An even better chance that all those romantic thoughts he'd been thinking when he'd prepared her breakfast had all just gone up in smoke.

Her hand shook when she accepted the cool wet washcloth he offered her. "I'm figuring checkout time just got bumped up an hour or two."

"Don't be a goof." Thoughts grim, he watched with concern as she wiped her mouth. "So. What's up, kid?"

She started to shake her head, then thought better of it. "Don't know. I suppose I...could have picked up a flu bug on the bus."

Okay. Logical explanation, but somehow Mac didn't think they were dealing with a case of the flu.

But if she wanted to play that game, fine. He'd give her time to decide to level with him.

"You came here by bus? From where? Never mind." What was he thinking? She was dog sick. Now was not the time for twenty questions. "We can talk later when you're feeling better. Think you're tummy's settled some?"

She closed her eyes. Considered. "I think so."

"Then let's get you back into bed."

"I cannot tell you how sorry I am about this," she said as he helped her to her feet and walked her back to the bedroom.

"Like you never held my head when I tossed *my* cookies?"

They had not been angels during their teens. They'd never done drugs and had rarely drunk before they'd become legal. There had been occasions, however, when they'd experimented with some homemade wine or tapped the keg a little too often at any number of parties that always cropped up in the spring around graduation time. Mac and J.T. had always gotten sick. She never had.

"In you go." He covered her up and helped her to lie back on the pillows.

And that's when he saw how hard she was working to hold back tears. His Shallie, who used to come to him all quiet and sad eyes and sometimes have bruises on her face and tell him she was fine. That nothing had happened. That she'd fallen out of bed. Or run into a door in the dark.

He'd known damn well, even as a kid, he'd known, that what she'd run into was her mother's fist, or a backhand from one of Joyce Malone's transient boyfriends.

"Honey, what's wrong?"

"Don't…be so nice to me. I…I don't deserve to ha-have you b-be so nice to me."

"Hey, hey. What kind of talk is that?" He eased a hip onto the bed beside her, brushed the hair back from her forehead as a huge tear leaked from the corner of her eye. "You're my buddy. I love you. There's nothing you could do to ever change that."

He tugged a tissue from the table by the bed and handed it to her. "You ready to tell me what's going on?"

She closed her eyes, looked away from him to the far side of the room, and he could see that a huge measure of pride was in play for her.

For him it was pure disappointment.

"Maybe later," he suggested, knowing she'd tell him when she was ready.

Still not looking at him, she nodded.

He squeezed her arm. "See if you can get some more rest. Snow pretty much shut things down during the night, so I'm not going anywhere for a while—at least not until the city crew finds its way to this end of town."

Then he pressed a kiss on her forehead and left her.

Puzzled. Concerned. Afraid that he knew what her problem was—dejected by what that meant to the future he'd plotted out for the two of them in the wee hours of the morning when he'd lain alone in his bed and let himself think about the prospect of a future with Shallie Malone.

When she came looking for him later, Mac was sitting on the sofa by the fire with his laptop, where he'd spent the past hour glaring at his screen and reading about various stages of pregnancy.

"You took down the tree," Shallie said inanely. Somehow, it made her a little sad. There was something about a Christmas tree—even one that had shed most of its needles—that lit a warm little glow inside her.

Odd, since she didn't remember many merry Christmases in her childhood, or even her adulthood, for that matter.

And she was just plain pathetic to be thinking about that now.

"I think that tree was violating about fifty fire codes," Mac said, watching her carefully. "It was way past its prime. That's what I get for putting it up the day after Thanksgiving."

"Some things never change," she said, working up a smile as she walked to an oversize leather chair that faced the sofa and was close to the fire. She sank down into it. "You're still the little boy who loves Christmas."

"So," he said after a long, very silent moment, "how are you feeling?"

There was no avoiding this conversation. "Foolish."

She curled her stocking feet up under her, tugged her sloppy red sweater down over the knees of her jeans and propped her injured wrist on the arm of the chair. And damn, if she didn't feel tears well up again.

She was not a weeper. Never had been. Pregnancy-induced hormones had become the bane of her existence. She hated this constant surge of emotion that seemed to lie just below the surface.

How had she gotten herself in this fix? By being stupid. That's how. Damn Jared Morgan. She'd loved him. At least, she'd thought she had…just as she'd thought he loved her. Until he'd started losing his temper over nothing. At first he'd just shove her a little. Then it had been a slap. Then it had gotten to be a whole lot more. Even if she hadn't caught him with another woman—the last straw—she'd been going to leave him.

Oldest, saddest story in the book. She'd fallen for an abuser and a cheat—just like her mother had. It was a pattern as old as time. Grow up and move away from an abusive situation and land in another one.

Well, she'd gotten out of it. But then she'd made things worse. Still feeling low and undesirable and angry and hurt a month after she'd ended things between them, she'd let her friends talk her into going out with them one night to a singles bar.

Just to get back among the living again.

Just to remember what it felt like to have a man look at her and not want to hit her.

It had been a little Band-Aid for her ravaged pride when the first man who had smiled at her made her feel like a woman again.

She'd needed his lies so badly. To ease the hurt. To fill the void. To salvage her self-esteem.

One night. One stupid, stupid night. When she'd awakened the next morning and had to face what she'd done, it was the lowest point in her life.

And then it had gotten even lower.

Brad Bailey of the charming smile and winning ways was just another cheater. Only, he'd been cheating on his wife.

Which had made Shallie feel like the biggest slug on the face of the earth.

The apple didn't fall so far from the tree after all, did it, Mom? she thought now, as she'd thought many, many times since that night.

And just like her mother, who Shallie had vowed she'd never become, now she was pregnant by a man she abhorred—not only for lying to her, but for what he'd done to his wife and family.

Like Shallie, the baby growing inside her may not have been conceived under ideal circumstances, but Shallie was determined to do the right thing by her child. She would not ignore her baby. She would not desert it. She would never hit her child, never make it feel like a mistake. No. She would not do any of the things her own mother had done to her.

This child would be loved. And this child would know it. Every day of her life, Shallie would make certain of that.

Shaking her head, she fought for control when she realized that Mac's worried gaze was focused intently on her. She didn't deserve his concern. But he did deserve the truth. At least, as much of the truth that she could bear to tell him.

"I'm pregnant," she said, figuring she'd just as well blurt it out and get it over with. Her heart beat like crazy while she waited for his reaction. When it came, it was the last one she'd expected.

"I know. I'm thinking about three months along?"

Her gaze shot to his. "How did you *know?*"

He lifted the laptop. Shrugged, trying o hide his concern. She saw it anyway. Along with he merest thread of anger…and worse. Disappointment. "I've been reading. You should be out of the morning sickness stage soon."

"No. I mean, how did you know I was pregnant?"

"Lucky guess?"

Shallie was horrified. "Is it that obvious?"

"Only to someone who knows you. Shallie," he said gently, "you refused pain medication last night for one thing. I wondered about it then. I mean, I know you're tough, but that went a little beyond making sense to me. And you turned down my best wine. Nobody turns down my wine."

He was trying to make her smile, but she just didn't have it in her at the moment.

"As for this morning," he continued, "I remember that cast-iron stomach of yours. When we were kids, I'd be barfing my guts out with the flu and you wouldn't so much as burp. So you and a case of the flu at nine in the morning didn't really seem like a good bet."

She sat in silence, waiting for questions or recriminations or something. Instead he seemed to be waiting for her to talk. So she did.

"This is the part where you're supposed to say something like, how could you be so careless? For Pete's sake, Shallie. Ever heard of birth control? Or—"

He cut her off with a raised hand. Seemed to gather

himself. Shrugged. "Like I said. I'm your friend. Not your judge. Now what can I do to help?"

She should have known that he'd respond with generosity instead of giving her grief. But then, he didn't know the whole story. If he did, he might not feel so generous.

Because of that…and because he was who he was—solid, steady and true—she felt like crying and laughing at the same time. So she did that, too.

"You could get me some of that tiramisu," she said after she'd dried her eyes.

He rose with a forced grin. He paused by her chair for a moment, then gently ruffled her hair as he walked by her on his way to the kitchen. "One order of tiramisu comin' right up."

"Better?" Mac sat across his kitchen's island counter and watched Shallie clean up the rich chocolate and butter finger dessert.

"Much. Chocolate *always* works."

He scooted off his stool and retrieved a carton of milk from the fridge. "Then I'm your man because there's lots more where that came from. In the meantime, drink some more milk. Good for you and for the kid."

"Yeah," she agreed. "Good for me and for the kid."

"The baby…it's okay and everything, right? I mean, hitting that snowbank. It didn't jar something loose, or hurt the baby?"

"Oh, Mac."

She must have been able to tell from his voice how much he'd been worried about that possibility, because she looked sad for him.

"No. Don't worry about the baby. The doctor checked me out. Everything's fine."

"Thank God." He heaved a breath of relief. It was bad enough he'd been responsible for breaking her wrist. If he'd caused any harm to her baby, well, he didn't know if he could live with that, too.

Just like he didn't know how he was going to live with the idea that she was probably still in love with the baby's father. After all, she'd cared enough about the guy to sleep with him. The Shallie he knew would have to care—even love a man—to get that deeply involved. And yet, she was here—which meant the jerk wasn't the man she'd thought he was.

Poor kid. And poor him.

Pipe dreams. Last night had been one big pipe dream.

She lapsed into silence while he made a big show of wiping down the counter. He needed something to do with his hands. He was determined to wait for her to talk—about the baby, about the father, who he'd already decided was a lying, cheating lowlife or she wouldn't have had a need to come back to Montana.

Yeah, he'd wait and see if she needed to talk about it. Or, if she wanted to just be quiet, that would be okay, too.

His resolve lasted all of a minute. "Okay," he said, turning back to her with a scowl. "So, where's the father? Why isn't he here? With you? Taking care of you?"

Nothing. Unless you counted the fact that her shoulders stiffened. That told him the issue of the father was a lot more than nothing.

"Is there some jerk out there somewhere who needs his lights punched out? Because I'm just the man to do it."

Her brown eyes met his over the glass of milk. She smiled, but it was a sad smile and it made his chest feel all squishy. "Thanks for offering."

Which meant, yeah, there was some creep who'd broken her heart and left her in a bad way. But she wasn't ready to share that piece of information with him. Probably because she knew he wasn't blowing smoke. Seeing her this way—miserable and pregnant and on her own—he was pretty much in love with the idea of making the guy pay with a little blood loss for leaving her in this fix.

Her mother hadn't given her anything but pain when she was a little girl. She didn't deserve more of it. Not from some guy who wasn't smart enough to know what he was giving up.

"Know anyplace that would be willing to hire a one-armed, pregnant woman?"

Okay. So he'd let her change the subject. Even though he still wanted, in the worst way, to ask if she was in love with the bastard.

"You're not going back to your teaching job?"

She flashed a tight smile. "Yeah. Well. Here's the deal. I…I fudged a little on that. There's no job to go back to."

He frowned. "You wanna run that by me again?"

She raised a shoulder, looked toward the window where the sun was glinting off the foot or so of new snow. "I no longer have a job."

"You got fired?" Even as he asked, he couldn't believe that was possible.

"Kind of came down to that, yeah."

Now he was really ticked. "Because you're pregnant?"

"Because I'm not *married* and pregnant. It's okay," she added, evidently seeing just how ticked he was.

And he was ticked. And at the same time relieved.

She wasn't married to the jerk. She wasn't *married*. He shouldn't have felt so much relief. He felt guilty because he did. And confused. Most of all confused because the truth was, he didn't figure into her situation in any way other than a shoulder to lean on.

That's what she needed from him now. That's what he'd be.

"I know I could fight it. And I'd probably win. The truth is, I don't want to fight. I don't want to go back there."

Her gaze drifted to the window. "I need to start fresh, you know? Me and my baby."

She smiled again, plucky to the bone. "Hadn't planned on job hunting with only one good wing, though."

Yeah. There was that. Guilt settled on his shoulders, as heavy as last night's snowfall. "Thanks to me."

"Oh—I didn't mean that. It was just the luck of the draw. Don't worry about it. I've got a little savings stashed away. I'll get by until I can work again. It won't be *that* long."

Mac rose, poured himself a cup of coffee and thought about the idea that suddenly popped into his head. "Tell you what," he said, deciding it was the perfect solution. "I know where there's a place available. The rent should be cheap, too."

She perked right up. "Yeah? Where?"

"The old Fremont cabin," he said, figuring she didn't

need to know he owned it, because knowing Shallie she'd figure she would be taking advantage of him if she stayed there.

"Ah. You mean *your* cabin."

He scowled over his mug. So much for her not knowing he owned the cabin. "Bob Coleman really has got a big mouth."

"Your name is on the mailbox."

Oops. "Right. Forgot about that. Regardless, the only reason I bought it was so I'd have a place to sleep when I'm in Sundown, working on the Dusk to Dawn. You'd actually be doing me a favor if you stayed there. Keep an eye on things, you know? This way I won't have to worry if the electricity goes off or the furnace goes on the fritz."

"You're worried about the furnace?"

"Okay, well, no. I had a new one put in this fall, but winter is winter. You never know."

She shook her head. "You're fabricating excuses to make me feel like I'm not imposing. Look, Mac, this is very sweet—and so are you," she added, her eyes soft, "but I'm not going to take advantage of your friendship—"

"Take advantage…please," he pleaded giving up on the pretense of her doing him a favor. He wanted her close. He didn't want her so close, however—like in the bedroom across the hall—that he'd be tempted to…hell. What would he be tempted to do?

She was pregnant. And he was probably right—she was most likely still in love with the creep who was responsible—and if she was, Mac really didn't want to know.

The hell he didn't.

And that realization added a bone-deep ache, to go with the anger that was knotting his gut.

"Look," he said, just to keep things in perspective, "the cabin is just sitting there empty most of the time. I rarely use it, and if I need to stay there sometime, it's not like there isn't room for both of us."

"But it's your home."

He lifted a hand in a gesture that encompassed the kitchen. "*This* is my home. The cabin is a convenience. I only bought it because I knew I'd be splitting my time between Sundown and Bozeman until I got the Dusk to Dawn running the way I want it."

He expelled a patient breath. "Now at the risk of sounding redundant, you are my friend. Let me do this for you. Come on," he wheedled, flashing his most persuasive smile. "Just say yes, for Pete's sake. I'm dying of guilt, here, for putting you in that cast."

She frowned into her glass of milk. But he could tell she was coming around.

"You have to let me pay you something."

Like hell. "Fine. Whatever. We'll work that out later."

"Okay," she said finally. "But just until I'm released to do some kind of work."

"We'll worry about that later, too."

She studied her fingers as she ran them up and down the glass of milk. "That's something I've gotten pretty good at—worrying about things later. One of these days, I'm going to have to figure something out."

Poor little short-stack, Mac thought. She really has had a lot on her plate to deal with.

"Well, that day isn't today," he said softly. "Today is all about you getting rested up and me making sure that you do."

One corner of her mouth tipped up. "Anyone ever tell you you've got a major mother complex?"

"Bite your tongue. I'm all man. And I've got the tools to prove it." He shook a finger at her when her burst of surprised laughter told him the direction her mind had taken on that one.

"*Hand* tools, Malone. They're in the drawer right next to my aprons."

She laughed again when he opened a drawer and pulled out a hammer and an apron with Kiss the Cook splashed across the front in bold red letters.

"God, I've missed you," she said in a voice that was warm with affection and a little sad with regret.

Yeah. He'd missed her, too. Just like it looked as if he'd missed his chance with her.

He pushed his little self-pity moment aside. She was the one with problems. He had the means to help her out. And making her smile was one of them. "You'll get over that soon enough. I'll make you sick of me in no time."

"Not likely."

No. It wasn't likely, Mac thought. He sure as hell knew he wasn't going to get sick of seeing her. Stressed over seeing her, he realized when, despite the disclosure of her pregnancy, she lifted her arms over her head and stretched, and her breasts pressed against that baggie red sweater. A sharp, direct tug of lust pulled straight from his chest to his groin.

That sweater. It was old and ratty and obviously well-worn and well loved. And until that uncalculated stretch, she looked about as shapeless as a sack of spuds in it.

But he knew that wasn't the case. He knew that her breasts were soft and full and warm underneath it. And as he watched her now, he had an in-your-face visual reminder.

"Mac?"

His name registered on a level that told him she might be repeating it.

"Yeah? Hmm? What?"

He dragged a hand over his face and avoided her questioning brown eyes.

Smooth, McDonald. Real smooth.

"Where'd you go?" she asked with a curious grin as she slipped off the stool that flanked the island.

"Maui," he said, deadpan. "Those quick trips do wonders for cabin fever. What did I miss while I was gone?"

Another smile. "I asked you how long you've had Spaghetti Western."

"Tell you what. You go sit by the fire. Since chocolate seems to settle, I'll make us some cocoa and be right with you. I'll tell you all about it."

And while she was in the living room, he'd putzed around making that cocoa until he had his head back on his shoulders where it belonged—instead of in his pants where it was giving him ten kinds of trouble.

Four

Half an hour later, Shallie hugged one arm around her waist and sipped her cocoa while she stood by Mac's huge picture window and watched him clean off his driveway. Snow flew in a big, high arc as the snow blower cut through the foot-deep snow and ate an ever-widening path on the concrete.

She couldn't help but smile. He was right about the all-man part. He was out there working in his jeans, a plaid flannel shirt and a black down vest. Boots and a pair of gloves were the only other concessions he'd made to the cold. Nothing on his head. No scarf around his neck. No jacket to cut the bitter winter cold.

His nose and cheeks were red with it. Frost puffed out of his mouth like smoke as he worked his way back and forth on the driveway. The women must still drool all over him, she thought, remembering the way the girls used to swarm around him in high school. Mac and J.T. both, with their rugged good looks and quick, teasing grins, had broken more hearts than Montana had mountain peaks.

He had that undeniable air of competent male about him. It was there in the way he carried himself. In the way he smiled. In the way he related to people. Competent, confident, in charge. And he had integrity to spare. He was a guy's guy. And he was a woman's dream man.

Why hadn't Jason been like Mac? Honest. Credible. Fun. True blue. And why had she had to meet Brad? Who cheated on his wife.

She always fell for the losers. And now she was one, too.

Mac was so much a winner. She'd bet he was still breaking hearts—then had the proof of her suspicions when his phone rang. She was about to open the door and tell him he had a call when the message on his answering machine kicked on.

"Hey, it's Mac. Leave a message."

"Hi, sexy man. It's Lana. I was hoping I'd catch you at home."

The voice was seductive and kitten soft and had Shallie rolling her eyes and feeling like an eavesdropper. Which she was. She was also very curious and—now here was an admission that shocked her—a little jealous.

She should leave the room, she thought, glancing over her shoulder at the phone. But she couldn't quite make herself move as the voice purred on.

"Anyway, you haven't called in ages," Lana continued, sounding a little pouty, "so I thought I'd see what you've been up to. We could do drinks sometime. I'm dying to see your new place."

Oh, I'll just bet you are, Shallie thought with a snort.

"Hey," Lana of the midnight-velvet voice continued, "here's a thought. New Year's Eve is just four days away. So, call me, baby. We could ring in the New Year together. I'll show you a real good time, I promise. Bye-ee."

"Bye-ee," Shallie mimicked, picturing Lana as a voluptuous, if slightly needy, blonde and wondering if she was one of Mac's half-a-brain dates.

That thought was funny for all of a moment.

Speaking of half-a-brain. Who was she to judge?

She was twenty-seven years old. She was broke. She was three months pregnant and on the run from a relationship that never should have been.

In short, she was not exactly living the lofty dream she'd had when she'd left Sundown ten years ago. She had been going to be somebody. She had been going to make a difference.

And look at her now.

Shallie looked down at her still-flat tummy and gently covered it with her good hand. "So, what do you think of your momma so far, little one?"

I'm guessing, not so much, she thought on a deep sigh.

"Don't you worry, baby mine," she promised in a soft whisper. "We've just hit a little bump in the road. It'll be okay. We'll be okay. I promise. I'm not going to let you down."

And that's how Mac found her.

She was standing in a shaft of light that angled in from his front window. The sun kissed the rim of her cheekbones, cast glossy highlights on her soft-brown curls.

Her hand covered her tummy. Her voice was whisper soft and reassuring.

He must have cleared his throat or something because, startled, she turned her head abruptly to look at him. Her brown eyes were bright, her lips tipped up into a smile that said she was happy to see him.

And, damn, he thought, as his heart kicked him a couple of good ones in the chest, if she wasn't one of the prettiest sights he'd ever seen.

"Hey, hard-working man," she said, her eyes filling with a wicked light. "You got a phone call while you were outside."

He tucked his gloves into his hip pockets then shrugged out of his vest. "Who was it?"

"La-na," she said, drawing out the name on a breathy, theatrical sigh. "She left a message. Sounds like you're gonna get lucky. She promised you a reallll gooood time."

Mac snorted. "Lana promises everybody a real good time," he said, wishing he'd never gotten involved with her last year. You live. You learn.

"You up for a ride?" he asked, wanting to change the subject. Lana, like most of the women he'd dated, left a lot to be desired in the "real person" department. Why did women have to play so many games? Why couldn't they just be themselves? Be honest, for Pete's sake instead of devious to the point of deceitful? You couldn't trust one of them. Even his own mother, it turned out, had been a liar and a cheat.

Shallie. Now, there was a woman you could count on. Too bad she didn't want to count on him for anything more than friendship.

"Most of the main streets should be cleared by now," he said, damn grateful that the woman sharing his house at the moment didn't have a deceitful bone in her body. "I need to check on some things at the restaurant. We can have lunch while we're there."

"You can't go on feeding me."

"Why not? I feed half of Bozeman on a good weekend."

"Half of Bozeman *pays* for the pleasure."

"Half of Bozeman is not my good friend. What's the point of having a restaurant if I can't feed my friends?

"Look," he added when he could see she wasn't convinced, "if you were gainfully employed—which you aren't, thanks to yours truly—and you could pay your way, it would be different."

She walked into the kitchen and rinsed her cup in the sink. "Would it?"

"No, actually, it wouldn't," he admitted. "I'd still want to feed you for free, only you wouldn't think anything of it."

She glanced at him over her shoulder, then laughed. It was a great sound.

"Your logic totally escapes me," she said turning back to him.

"It's only when a person is unable to do something that they feel like they need to do it," he explained. "So, following that logic, if you were flush, and paying for dinner wasn't a problem, you wouldn't feel bad about accepting it free."

She opened her mouth. Shut it. Shook her head. "I'm not going to win this argument, am I?"

"Now you've got it," he said, and, acting on impulse, turned her around to face him and plopped a kiss on her forehead. She smelled fresh and warm and new. And sexy as ever-loving sin.

Pregnant, he reminded himself. The lady is pregnant.

"So…are you up for it?" he asked again. "And just so you know, the answer to that question is yes."

"Well then, yes," she said on a laugh.

"Cool," he said. "Whenever you're ready."

"Umm—" she made a gesture toward the phone "—what about La-na?"

He shrugged back into his vest. "What about her?"

"Aren't you going to call her back?"

"I'll get around to it…one of these days."

She grinned.

He'd like to think that maybe it was because Shallie was a little pleased that he wasn't going to call Lana back. Wishful thinking, McDonald.

"You're a bad man, Brett McDonald."

"I'm a *single* man," he stated with playful conviction. Shallie had spoiled him for any other woman. "And in spite of Lana's agenda, I plan to stay that way." Because the woman he wanted didn't have a clue that he loved her.

It hurt suddenly. Accepting that, after all these years, he still loved Shallie Malone, and the possibility of her loving him back was the same now as it had been back then. Zip.

"Besides, I'm going to be an uncle," he added, gently patting her tummy to project the illusion that all was fine and dandy in his world. "I'll have duties. No time for wild women because I'll be taking the little guy to the park, teaching him how to fish."

He could see in her eyes that she'd needed that small assurance that she wasn't going to be going through this alone. That he was going to be there for her and for her baby.

And he would be. He made that promise to himself as much as to her right then and there.

"Him?" she asked, her brown eyes glistening with speculation.

"Him. Her. Doesn't matter. Kid still needs to know how to fish. Now, come on. Grab your jacket and let's boogie. We'll talk about names on the way. I'm kind of partial to Heathcliff and Gertrude. Whadaya think?"

"Oh, man." Three nights later Mac sat back from his dining room table with a blissful look on his face. "Shallie, you give me the recipe for this cheesecake and not only will that running tab you insist on keeping, of what you think you owe me, be wiped clean, I'll end up owing *you* money."

Sitting at Mac's huge mission oak dining room table, three whole days after she'd arrived, Shallie grinned, watching him polish off the cheesecake she'd topped with a sugary raspberry sauce. "I'm thinking that means you like it."

"Like it? Honey, I'm crazy for it. What a proud moment. My little short-stack grew up and learned how to make something other than PBJs."

He was good at making her smile. He was just plain good for her, Shallie thought, not for the first time since she'd been staying with him.

And not for the first time she thought about what it would be like to be Brett McDonald's woman. The word *easy* came to mind. And just like that, the thought went away.

Don't trust *easy,* she mentally repeated the mantra that had proven itself true too many times in her life.

"I'm serious," he continued. "I'd kill for this recipe. How did you manage it, anyway—not just dessert but the entire dinner, which was awesome, by the way. How did you do it? I mean, with your arm and all?"

Grilling the salmon and making a salad hadn't been that difficult. And while it had been a bit of a trick to whip up the cheesecake with only one fully functional hand, Shallie had learned how to manage a lot of things in the past three days.

"It's all about leverage," she said. "And determination. Oh, yeah—and your state-of-the-art kitchen, gadgetman."

He leaned back in his chair, balancing on two of its legs, and waggled his eyebrows. "Like my toys, do ya?"

She laughed. "Oh, yeah. I like your *kitchen* toys." And she was happy that he'd enjoyed the meal she'd prepared for him. She'd been determined to make him something special after all he'd done for her.

"As to the recipe, it's all yours," she told him. "And small payment for such exceptional room and board."

He let his chair drop back down to all fours. Gave her a stern look. "Okay. Let's not spoil this kick-ass meal by forcing me to go into lecture mode. You owe me nothing. Nada. Zip. As a matter of fact, you just did me a huge favor. I was going to go back to the restaurant and work tonight, but now that I'm feeling full and lazy, I think I'll knock off for the night."

"You work too hard," she said.

"Damn straight," he agreed without any real conviction, unclipped his cell phone from his belt and punched in a number. "Cara. Hi. It's Mac. What's happening?"

Shallie watched while he nodded, answered some questions from Cara Brown, his night manager.

He did work too hard, whether he wanted to admit it or not. Mac, she'd discovered, was a very hands-on manager. Did everything from cooking to bartending to maintenance, if the need arose. He put in a lot of hours at the restaurant during the past three days she'd been staying with him.

Three days. Amazing. Shallie wasn't sure how it had happened, but the time had passed in a blur. She'd rested and was recovering from not only the broken wrist but from the past few months of stress and worry about her future.

Mac had a way of making everything but the moment seem to be in another realm. A realm that was not really part of the here and now. Like tonight, for instance.

He'd breezed in the door about six, after calling and telling her he'd come to pick her up and take her to the restaurant for dinner, as he had every night. When they'd gone grocery shopping that morning, she hadn't told him that she'd made certain to pick up the items for this surprise, special dinner.

"Sounds like you've got things well in hand," Shallie heard him say after he and his manager had apparently covered all the bases. "Listen. I'm going to call it a day. Give me a ring if something comes up. I can be there in five minutes. Yeah. Thanks. G'night.

"Done deal," he said after he'd hung up. "I'm yours for the night."

She shook her head at his big grin. And fought the urge to wish she really was his. He was so special, this man. Funny. Sexy. Tender, and yet as alpha as they came.

The question was out before she could stop it. "So why aren't you someone *else's* for the night? Someone like Lana?" she added with a teasing waggle of her eyebrows to hide how curious she really was.

"Don't you worry about Lana. The fact is, she's just not my type." He rose and started clearing up the table. And, if she didn't miss her guess, to run away from this line of questioning. Interesting.

"You cooked," he said, gathering dishes for the dishwasher, "I'll clean up."

Shallie stood, too, and followed him into the kitchen with her plate and silverware. And her seriously piqued curiosity. "So what kind of woman *is* your type?"

He shot a glance over his shoulder. "Anyone ever tell you that you're nosy, Ms. Malone?" He sounded more amused at her line of questioning than upset by it—and maybe he also sounded a little nervous. Interesting.

"More than one. You'd think I'd learn. So, why *isn't*

there a special woman in your life, *Mr.* McDonald?" She couldn't help it. Now that she'd opened up this channel, she wanted to know. "I mean, it's not like you're mud ugly or anything—"

"Aw shucks, thank you, ma'am." He winked at her as he opened the dishwasher and stacked their plates.

"And then there's that humble bumpkin thing you've got going for you," she added with a smile. "Plus, you're a nice guy. You're financially solvent—and then some—and unless you've switched teams while I've been gone, you're arrow straight."

"Same team," he assured her and made a show of flexing his bicep. "I jus' *luvs* the ladies."

She laughed. "And I'm sure the ladies jus *luvs* you. So, really—why haven't you gotten married? And don't give me that ring-in-the-nose bit because I'm not buying it."

He waited long enough that she was beginning to wonder if he was going to tell her to take a hike. Finally he turned back to her.

"Okay, here's the deal," he said, tossing a dish towel over his shoulder. Leaning back against the counter, he crossed his ankles then folded his arms over his broad chest. "I like my life. I like calling my own shots. I like doing what I want to do, when I want to do it. I like not having to be responsible for anyone but me. And most of the women I know, well, let's just say they leave a lot to be desired in many areas," he added, his eyes growing hard. "Besides, from my perspective, marriage, as an institution, isn't all it's cracked up to be."

She figured he was referring to his parents. Figured also—more from what he hadn't said than what he had said—that their divorce may have soured him. But the Mac she knew was also a cockeyed optimist. It was hard to believe he'd just written off marriage.

She eased a hip onto a bar stool, leaned her elbow on the granite countertop. "How do you know that, if you don't give it a chance?"

He considered, then pinned her with a look. "Did you? Did you give the institution of marriage a chance?"

Okay. Ouch. Not only had she not given marriage a chance, she'd almost been responsible for breaking up one. And that was something she would always have to live with.

A familiar sinking nausea accompanied that reality—and it had nothing to do with a biological reaction from her pregnant hormones. It was about shame. About being stupid and needy and so blinded by the humiliation Jared had caused her that she'd rushed headlong into a situation with Brad that added mortification to the mix.

She was not a home wrecker. And as soon as she'd found out she was pregnant, she'd made up her mind that Brad would never know about the baby. This baby was hers. She would raise it. Love it. Take care of it.

"Shallie? You okay?"

When she realized she'd been a couple of thousand miles and two months ago away, she pulled herself back to the moment. What was done was done. She couldn't undo it. But she could not bring herself to level with Mac about the truth surrounding her baby's conception. She knew that he assumed the father had abandoned her. She knew it was wrong the let him continue to think it. But she couldn't bear to see the disappointment in his eyes if he knew the whole story.

Which meant that she really needed to stop prying into his business since she hadn't confided the whole truth about hers to him.

"I'm fine—other than being a prying bore. Sorry. Your love life is none of my business."

An odd look that she couldn't read crossed his face.

"Tell you what," he said, tossing the dish towel over the edge of the sink and pushing away from the counter, "what do you say we let our relationship issues drop and see if we can find a movie on pay per view? I bought that monster of a flat screen when I moved in and I don't think I've watched it for more than an hour total—and that's been in fits and starts."

"Deal," she said, because she really did want him to just kick back and relax since that's what a night off should be about. "Just no blood-and-gore flick, okay?"

"You used to *love* blood and gore," he pointed out with a disappointed frown.

"And I will again—just not at this particular stage of my pregnancy."

"Ah. Got it. Does that mean we have to watch a chick flick?"

"Not my cuppa, either, at the moment."

In the end they compromised. They found an old Steve Martin comedy and, snuggled on the couch with a fire glowing in the hearth and a very light snow feathering down, laughed their way through it.

* * *

When Mac woke up several hours later, his arm was asleep. His neck had a crick in it. The TV droned softly, and a soft, warm and amazingly sexy woman was snuggled up against him.

Shallie.

For a long moment he just lay there, absorbing her heat, enjoying the moment. He didn't remember falling asleep. He sure didn't remember stretching out full length on the sofa and taking sleeping beauty with him for the ride.

But evidently he had, because he was flat on his back and Shallie was plastered against his side like a second skin, the weight of her cast lying heavily on his chest. The weight of her thigh, however slight, was settled with a much more pronounced effect across his lap. A lap that was suddenly reacting to all this soft woman heat sleeping by his side.

Perfect. Be a guy. Embarrass the hell out of both of us.

Or fix it. Fast, lunkhead.

So, as he'd sometimes had to make himself do the past three days when he found himself caught up in some unsolicited and inappropriate sexual fantasy about Shallie, he thought of anything but all that heat.

Tax audits. Quarterly payments. The waitress schedule. The reservation for the Simpsons' wedding rehearsal dinner that was going to be a nightmare to pull together. The leaky roof at the Dusk to Dawn that was going to cost a small fortune to fix.

And let's not forget, this is a pregnant woman you're holding in your arms.

Okay. That helped. Enough, at least, that he could draw another breath—but not an easy one.

Careful not to disturb her, he yawned hugely, then checked his watch. Holy cow. It was almost 2:00 a.m. He needed to get her to bed where she could get some quality rest. But then she stirred, and his arm automatically tightened around her back, sliding instinctively down her hip to hold her so she wouldn't tumble to the floor.

Lordy, she was small. Slight, fine bones. Slim, lean curves. But curves, just the same. Why had he never realized before how fragile she was?

Because of her grit, that's why. Tough. Shallie Malone had always been tough. She'd had to be.

He remembered the first time he'd ever seen her. She'd been all of eleven years old. She'd shown up at school near the end of the spring semester. Her clothes had been worn and patched and not all that clean. Her hair had been just as curly then as it was now, only it had stuck out around her face like a Raggedy Ann doll.

The Griener twins had cornered her on the playground at recess and had been giving her the new-kid-in-town third-degree.

"Where'd ya get them jeans? Looks like a clown wore 'em they've got so many patches," Billy Griener had said, acting superior and mean.

"Yeah," Willie had chimed in. "Got clown hair, too. Do a trick, clown."

"Yeah, clown, do a trick," Billie ordered on a mean laugh.

"I'll do a trick," the new girl had said. "See how you

like this one." Then she'd walked up to Willie and kneed him in the groin.

Mac smiled into the dark, remembering. Willie had howled like a scalded dog all the way to the teacher, who had promptly dragged Shallie to the principal's office.

Mac and J.T. had been waiting for her on the steps when school got out that day.

"What do you want?" she'd snarled, her little hands clenched into fists at her sides, the set of her mouth telling him she was ready to take on the world if she had to.

Mac had only been a kid himself, but he'd figured out then and there that Shallie Malone had probably taken on the world several times already in her short life. And if he hadn't already fallen in love with her, he did right then.

"I want to shake the hand of the girl who put wailing Willie to his knees," he'd said.

She'd looked suspicious at first, but then he'd grinned at her and stuck out his hand. "And I want to make sure I'm on your good side, 'cause I don't ever want to see your knee comin' at me the way it came at Willie."

Still uncertain, she drew back her shoulders but cautiously shook his hand.

"What about you?" She'd turned a dark look on J.T.

"You play baseball?" J.T. asked with a matching scowl.

"I can play circles around you," she'd said, her chin notching up, daring him to dispute her claim.

J.T. had grinned. "Cool. Let's go to the park and get us a game going. We'll whump the snot out of anyone who thinks they can beat us. You'll be our ringer."

That was all it had taken to melt her ice block of resistance. And aside from it being his first puppy love crush, the three of them had been fast friends from that day on.

If anyone ever needed a friend, it had been Shallie. Joyce Malone, Shallie's mom, had drifted into town, Mac had heard eavesdropping one day at the Dusk to Dawn, because she'd needed a place to hide out from a string of bad debts and bad relationships.

For whatever reason, Joyce had taken a liking to Sundown, and that's where she and Shallie had stayed, until Shallie had graduated from high school. Shortly after Shallie left, Joyce hooked up with a trucker and took off, too.

Mac had never liked Joyce Malone. Not just because of the physical bruises she sometimes put on Shallie. The emotional bruises were just as hard for his little short-stack to deal with. Both his mom and J.T.'s mom had always had time for the three of them underfoot. They'd always had cookies, too. And hugs when they'd needed them. Most likely they were the only hugs Shallie had ever gotten, Mac figured, because Shallie never took them home to see *her* mother. And she never had much to say about her.

"She's workin'," Shallie would say with a look that dared anyone to dispute it.

Truth was, Mac had figured out when he was old enough to learn the way it was with women like Shallie's mom, that in between her job at the dry cleaners,

Joyce Malone did a lot of work on her back. On more then one occasion, he or J.T. had had to wipe a smirk off one of their brainless buddies' faces when they'd suggested that maybe Shallie did a little back work herself for Mac and J.T.

She stirred again, and the warmth of her breath tickled his throat. His body reacted when her thigh slid across his lap. The sweet friction almost made him groan. And when the swell of her breast pressed oh, so sweetly against his chest, he thought he might dive right off the deep end.

Okay. Time to nip this little disaster-in-the-making in the bud.

Five

"Shallie." Mac whispered softly so he wouldn't startle her. "Sweetheart. Wake up. We need to hit the sack."

She sighed and nestled closer, her cheek resting on his shoulder. "Mmm. Okay. In a minute."

He lay rock still. Except for his heart, which was pounding so hard in reaction to her silky sigh and soft body that he was certain the reverberation would wake her up.

But she was asleep again. Or so said her deep, even breaths.

He was far from asleep. He'd dreamed about holding her like this for years. And now here she was. In his arms—yet just as unattainable as she had been all those years ago.

Lord help him.

"Shallie," he whispered, determined to do the right

thing. "Come on, sleepyhead. You're going to get all stiff and sore lying mashed against me like this."

"Comfy," she breathed, and shifted again and damned if all of her didn't somehow end up on top of all of him. "So…comfy."

Well, hell. Because the trouble was, it *was* comfy. Damn comfy. He could feel so much more of her now, and the weight was wonderful. Her breasts pressed firmly against his chest, and with a little imagination he could picture her nipples pressing against her bra. And of course that picture stirred up more and more pictures. Like the two of them skin on skin and him sinking deep inside of her.

He wasn't just rock still now, he was rock hard, too. And, Lord help him, she had to be able to notice.

She'd kill him. She'd flat-out kill him. Neuter him with that lethal knee if nothing else. And he'd deserve it.

He held his breath. Waited for her to lift her head, glare at him and tell him to grow up.

But she didn't. She did something else, instead. And he had to believe she was still half-asleep because never in a million years would a wide-awake and alert Shallie start moving her thigh back and forth along his erection as if she not only didn't hate that it had sprung up between them, but like she liked—more than liked—the way it felt against her.

Sweet heaven, he needed some of the blood that had shot to his groin to find its way north and fuel a little gray matter.

"Shallie," he groaned, feeling himself losing the battle with his better judgment.

She moved again with an answering little sigh, pushing herself higher, rubbing her breasts and her belly against him as she lifted her head and touched her mouth to his.

Mother.

He needed to push her away. Clearly, she didn't know what she was doing. Except she sure *acted* as if she knew, and she was doing it damn well. Maybe she was awake after all. Maybe…maybe she did feel something for him. Maybe she was as hot for him as he was for her.

Her lips were sure as hell hot, and so incredibly soft against his. And when that tentative contact of her closed mouth slowly transitioned to the sound of a yearning sigh and she opened for him, he ran out of reason and will to fight it.

He was only so strong. How could he not welcome her open kiss? Devour her questing tongue when she slid it along his teeth, then slipped inside.

Hunger. Yearning. Need. It was all there. And he fed it. His and hers. Catered to it. Built on it, wrapping her tightly against him and fusing his mouth to hers.

Heaven above, she tasted fine. Felt even better. The inside of her mouth was hot and slick. Her body was both lean and lush; her hair was like silk when he buried one hand in her tangled curls. And he was barely aware of his own actions as he slipped the other up and under her sweater.

More heat. Heat to the point of burn when skin met skin and she arched into his hand. Before he knew what he was doing, he slid his hand up along her ribs and higher to find the weight of a full, heavy breast. He swallowed her gasp of pleasure when he gently squeezed. And when he flicked his thumb over the lace that covered her nipple, she pressed into his touch, driving him deeper into her fire. So deep, he rolled her beneath him and settled his weight fully on top of her.

He wedged his knee between her thighs, simply had to get closer. He had to touch more. He had to... *Whoa.*

He had to stop. That's what he had to do.

This was insane.

This was Shallie. Half-asleep. Totally vulnerable. Completely off-limits.

Pregnant.

He didn't know where he found the strength, but he slowly dragged his hand out from under her sweater. Slower still, he pulled his mouth away from hers, fighting her kitten sounds of protest.

Fueled by guilt and desire, his heart was pulsing at about one hundred per when he pressed her face against his neck and held her. Just held her, groping for brotherly thoughts, praying she wouldn't hate him when she came fully awake and realized what had just happened.

Maybe he'd get lucky, he thought, gently stroking her hair. Maybe she'd slept through the entire thing and she wouldn't even remember.

But then he felt her stiffen beneath him. Felt the flutter of her eyelashes against his throat and knew he could kiss that notion goodbye.

"Well." Her voice sounded husky; her breath was kind of thready. "This is…awkward."

Awkward. Good word.

So was *incredible.*

Amazing.

Hot.

Oh, and here was a word: *suicidal.* At least it would be if he pulled that train of thought any further. Time for a little diversionary drivel to get the train back on the right track.

He lifted his head. Frowned down at her. "Okay, lady. Who are you? And what have you done with my friend, Shallie?"

Thank you, God, her mouth turned up in a smile.

"I'm going to start counting," she said in her best hypnotist's voice, gamely playing along, "and when I reach ten, you will wake up, no longer have the urge to quack like a duck, and you will forget this ever happened."

Not damn likely.

Still, he forced a grin. She was cool with this. They were cool. Well, technically he was still hot, but he'd deal with that later.

"Okay. Just one last quack. Maybe two," he said then pushed out two very anemic quacks that actually had her giggling. "Now that I got that out of my system…umm…damn, Shall. I am so, so sorry."

"You should be sorry. No self-respecting duck sounds like that."

He pushed out a snort. "I was referring to what happened between us just now."

Her eyes softened. "I know."

He watched her face, looking for anger, relieved when he saw none. "I really *am* sorry."

He would go to hell for lying, too, because the truth was, he couldn't muster up the necessary regret to be sorry about anything right now. The kiss had been incredible. "Guess we…uh, both fell asleep."

"And woke up next to a warm, snuggly body," she added with a nod.

"And naturally, instinct took over—"

"And what with our weakened mental capacity and all," she continued.

"The next thing you know…yada, yada, yada." He was doing his damnedest to keep this light, when the situation was anything but. It was explosive, but again she kept the fire from burning out of control when she smiled. "Or something like that."

She searched his eyes for the longest time. "For the record, McDonald, you yada very well when you're asleep."

Ah. So that was why she was being so forgiving. She thought *he'd* been sleeping when this started, too.

It was a straw and he grasped it.

"Right back atcha, kid," he said lamely, shoving back the guilt, and finally had the presence of mind to haul his sorry self off her.

Maybe it was because he was tired. Maybe it was because, like most men, he was born horny. Maybe he was just a jerk. Whatever the reason, as he stood there looking down on her, he was fresh out of reasons why he shouldn't just pile back on top of her sweet, soft body and finish what her sleepy, sexy eyes told him she wouldn't mind finishing. And that was probably just more wishful thinking on his part.

So he did what any self-respecting jerk would do in this situation. He bailed.

"Before this gets any weirder…I'm hitting the sack. You sure you're okay with…uh…you know?"

She nodded. "I'm okay."

"All right. Well. G'night, then, short-stack. See you tomorrow."

Then he hightailed it the hell away from her before yada, yada, yada turned into hotter, hotter, hotter and they both woke up naked and way more than embarrassed in the morning.

The next night was New Year's Eve. Spaghetti Western was standing-room only. Had been since about 6:00 p.m. when locals and out-of-towners had decided to start their evening early with a nice dinner before they either went on to parties or home to watch the crystal ball drop in Times Square on TV.

And finally, finally, Shallie was able to do something to help Mac out. His regular hostess was down with a bad sinus infection. His back-up was on a ski trip to Steamboat. And Mac had already pressed any additional staff into action to help cover the rush.

"I can do it," Shallie had said that morning, sitting at the island in the kitchen after she'd overheard Mac on the phone to his day manager. "I can fill in as hostess," she told him when he'd hung up.

"I can't ask you to do that," he'd insisted.

"Why? Because I'm pregnant? Sorry. That's a nonissue. Because of my wrist? Another nonissue. I don't need two hands to keep track of seating charts and to seat people."

He'd frowned, but she could tell he was considering the idea.

"If it's experience you're worried about," she'd continued, determined to do this for him, "I paid my way through college working in restaurants. I've done everything from cooking to waiting tables to busboy chores to playing hostess. And I've spent enough time around SW these past few days that I have a pretty good feel for how things flow there.

"Besides," she'd added, resorting to the big guns when he'd still looked dubious, "I'm bored. Let me help. It'll be fun."

"I don't know." He'd still hedged.

"Please," she'd wheedled in a really good imitation of a woman about to throw a little temper tantrum.

"Oh, for Pete's sake. If you're going to get all sulky about it."

She'd seen the grin through his grousing and rushed over to give him a one-armed hug. "Thanks. It'll be great. You'll see."

It was the first time they'd touched since the "nocturnal kissing" incident the night before. And since then, Mac had made it a point to keep his distance. Shallie had done the same. Which was silly, she thought now as, despite her cast, she felt festive and even a little pretty in her red velvet holiday dress, while she ushered an elderly couple to a table.

"Enjoy your meal," she said with a smile, and handed them their menus.

So they'd fallen asleep, woken up in each other's arms and let their bodies do the talking before their brains had engaged, she thought, walking back to the hostess station. It wasn't as if it had been planned.

And it was silly to be thinking about that kiss now, Shallie told herself as she caught a glimpse of Mac. He was currently dug in behind the bar helping the bartender who was overrun with orders.

Still, it was hard for her not to think about it. He was an amazing kisser, her friend, Brett McDonald. His lips were so soft and skilled. And his body—Lord. She'd known he was in great shape. One look was all it had taken to figure that out. Chest to chest, hip to hip, however…well, tactile contact was much more telling than visual.

Much more telling, she thought, and actually felt her face flame hot when she remembered the feel of his hand on her breast and his very impressive erection pressing against her belly.

"You okay?" Cara, Mac's assistant manager, asked making a point to check on Shallie as she hurried by on the way to the dining room.

"Fine. Great," Shallie said quickly.

"Okay," Cara said with a concerned look. "You look a little flushed."

"Has Mac been telling you to watch out for me?" Shallie asked, all of a sudden more concerned that he might have inadvertently spilled the beans about her pregnancy than she was alarmed by the turn of her thoughts.

"Mac? He hasn't told me anything. You have a broken wrist. Seems to me that's enough reason to be a little concerned about you. Thought maybe you might have bumped it or something."

"Oh. Sorry." Shallie forced a smile. "I'm fine. No problems, really." Unless you count the fact that she was having a sexual fantasy about her best friend, which was about as left field as waking up in his arms and thinking about kissing him every time she saw him. "I'm having a good time. Am I doing okay?"

"You're doing great. In fact, you've been a godsend. We'll have three tables bussed and ready in a couple of minutes."

As Cara took off at a fast walk, Shallie glanced at the crush by the door and in the waiting area. They were talking and laughing, enjoying the complimentary champagne Mac had made available. No one seemed to mind the wait. Probably because they all knew a meal at SW was worth waiting for.

The rest of the night flew by. Shallie only caught glimpses of Mac as he worked the dining room, making certain everyone was happy and well fed and covered whatever base needed covering to make certain everything went smoothly. Yet every time their eyes met she felt a sharp little zing of arousal flashing between them.

It was unsettling and pulse-altering and…well, exciting. And she was totally wrong to be thinking about the possibility of something more happening between them.

She'd made a big enough mess of her life. She wasn't

going to mess it up further—or mess his up in the process. She made it a point to avoid eye contact the rest of the night and finally, around ten-thirty, the crowd had thinned to a few tables and the kitchen was in the process of shutting down. Shallie had just bidden two couples good-night and happy New Year when she realized Mac had slipped up beside her.

"Hey," he said with a tired smile. "How you holding up?"

"I'm great. Okay," she confessed when he narrowed his eyes, "my feet hurt a little. But it's been fun. Really. I enjoyed myself tonight."

"We couldn't have made it through the crush without you."

"You're overstating, but thanks for that."

"What do you say I grab something from the kitchen and we take it home to ring in the New Year with a late dinner?"

It was her turn to question him—first with a look, then with an admonishment. "It's New Year's Eve," she pointed out. "You don't have to babysit me."

"What are you talking about?"

"Don't you have a party or something to go to? A date waiting with a bottle of wine and a come-hither smile?" She didn't much like the idea that a woman might be waiting for him, but the truth was, it would be better all around if one was.

He grunted. "I've got a date with my sofa, and that's about as much action as I want after taking care of this crowd tonight."

"Really?" She felt too much relief over that news, but

pushed gamely on. "Because I'm okay if you just drop me off at the house."

"I'm not dropping you anywhere," he assured her. "Sit tight. I'll go raid the kitchen and tell Cara we're out of here. Be right back."

Shallie's nerves zinged like the zephyrs of wind that whisked powdery snow into tall, swirling gusts beneath the streetlights as Mac drove through town on deserted, winter-cold streets.

Get a grip, she told herself mentally. Just because this was New Year's Eve, the date night of all date nights, and she and Mac were together, it didn't mean anything.

But there are implications, the suddenly insane side of her personality reminded her.

Okay, *normally* there would be implications when two single people decided to spend one of the biggest holidays of the year together. There shouldn't, however, be any of that stuff in the mix between them.

And there wouldn't have been—except that last night had happened. Last night when they'd more than kissed. That spelled *implications* with a capital *I*. At least, it did from her perspective. Mac, however, didn't seem to be affected by the kiss at all.

Shallie glanced at him across the darkened cab of his truck. Nope. He seemed oblivious to her thoughts. Thoughts that had her looking at him through new eyes. The eyes of a woman as opposed to the eyes of a friend. And with a new awareness and appreciation of just how much of a man he was.

Careful, she warned herself. You've forgotten about

the *easy* factor. *Easy* spelled disaster for her. No matter how appealing this amazing man was.

He drove, she realized now, the way he did everything else. With confidence and complete control. Just as he was in complete control of whatever awkwardness he could have shown around her.

He was still quick with his smiles. Still attentive to a fault. And she hadn't seen a flicker of a notion that he felt any discomfort left over from last night.

Which was good, Shallie assured herself. It was a very good thing that one of them had their wits about them, she thought and, indulging herself in a wistful look at his poster-boy profile, she told herself to give it a rest.

She chalked up her lingering fascination with Mac, the man, to haywire hormones. It was the only logical explanation. She normally didn't cry, and she normally didn't have attacks of the hots for her best friend—who very clearly had forgotten all about the kiss that she was going to do her darnedest to put out of *her* mind, too.

She had much more critical items on her agenda, anyway. Items like finding a job and taking care of herself and her baby. And she'd made enough mistakes lately. She wasn't going to make a mistake with Mac— and if she repeated that particular mantra often enough, she just might pull it off.

If he didn't get his act together, Mac thought as he set the table for their late New Year's Eve dinner, he was going to fool around and screw up their friendship.

He may have been acting like a fool but he *wasn't*

one—at least, not normally. Well, damn, that dress she
had on tonight didn't help matters any.

It was bright-red velvet—a holiday dress—with long
sleeves that covered her cast, a deep-vee neckline and
a fitted and flirty short skirt. Man, he'd almost swallowed his tongue when she'd walked into the living
room with a smile and an "Will this be dressy enough
for the hostess at the hottest spot in Bozeman on New
Year's Eve?"

Oh, yeah. It was dressy enough. The hottest spot in
Bozeman that night, however had been anywhere she
had been. Her full breasts pressed provocatively against
the red velvet. Her tummy was still flat. And she had
the most amazing legs, not to mention sweet, curvy
hips that had had him salivating over the wet bar way
too often for a man his age.

He shook off the wallop of seeing her that way. Good
thing Shallie had her full wits about her. Half-wit was
about the most he could lay claim to, because he'd been
thinking about her in a totally man-woman way for the
better part last night and today.

All because of that kiss, she hadn't even been aware
that she'd initiated and then taken way beyond the ini-
tiation stage before he'd managed to put the skids on
his wayward libido. And before things had gotten completely out of hand.

It was the out-of-hand part he hadn't been able to get
out of his head. Another few minutes and he'd have had
her sweater off her. And damn it all…he'd been thinking
about that possibility way too much, also.

Well, it was clear that *she* wasn't thinking about it.

He was guessing the only thing she was thinking was that she was glad to be off her feet, that she was hungry as a bear and that it was way past time he fed her.

"You're stupid squared, that's what you are," he muttered while he debated—then against his better judgment—went ahead and lit the candles.

"Soup's on," he said as he walked into the great room where he'd ordered her to sit down in front of the fire with her feet up while he set out their meal.

"Smells like heaven," she said following him into the dining room. She stopped just inside the arched double doorway. "Oh. Oh, Mac. This looks wonderful."

"Let's hope it tastes good, too," he said, experiencing another one of those punches of lust when she smiled for him.

"For the lady." He made a grand gesture with a sweep of his hand and held her chair out for her. "Spinach salad, asparagus with cheese sauce and succulent Maine lobster. And for dessert, tiramisu. Oh," he added uncapping a bottle of sparkling white grape juice, "and a little nonalcoholic bubbly just for you to ring in the New Year."

Okay, he thought as he watched her face light up. Now he knew what it meant when someone said a woman looked radiant. Her eyes sparkled, her cheeks had turned a beautiful shade of carnation pink and, as tired as she had to be, there was a glow about her that made it appear she'd bathed in champagne.

And maybe he should have bitten the bullet and taken Lana up on her offer of a "really good time" because it was getting damn hot in here and he didn't have cooking privileges in Shallie's kitchen.

"This is all so special," Shallie said looking from her wineglass to the candles, then to him as he sat down across from her.

"It's New Year's Eve," he said with a brightness that he hoped to hell she didn't see through as his having a case of the hots for a woman he had no business being hot for. "And a special one at that when two old friends get together. So I figured we'd do it up right. Plus I thought you might be tired of eating Italian."

"I don't think I'd ever tire of the menu at SW," she said kindly. "You were so thoughtful to do this. As usual, it's too much."

"It's just right," he said, and snapped his napkin onto his lap. "Now, eat before it gets cold."

Cold. He should be so lucky.

"So," Mac said as they settled into the great room, him on the sofa, Shallie folded a safe distance away from him in a side chair, "my turn to play twenty questions."

She blinked, puzzled. "Your turn? When did I have *my* turn?"

"'What kind of woman is your type?' 'Why aren't you settled down?' 'Why aren't you married?'" he reminded her, mimicking her tone from the other day.

"Oh. *That* was my turn. I didn't know that. And I didn't know we were keeping track, but fair's fair." She grinned at him. "Okay. Shoot."

Oh, he planned to. During dinner he'd made some decisions. One: things had gotten just plain crazy from his perspective. So she was a gorgeous woman. So he'd always had a thing for her. Okay, more than a thing. So he'd always loved her. Still did, but that didn't really matter now. He had to cut it out. The overriding factor here was that all she needed him to be for her was a friend. So that's what he'd be. Period. Done deal.

Two: this sort of undercut the first issue, but he was now very interested in knowing what kind of man flipped her switch. And it wasn't a pride thing, he assured himself. He was curious, that was all. It wasn't as if his ego had taken a hit, knowing that the only time he had any male-female effect on her was when she was sleeping.

Okay. So maybe it *was* an ego thing. And maybe he didn't like knowing that he was jealous as hell of a man he didn't know. A man she was probably still in love with.

"You said something about a question?"

He looked up to see her waiting, with a curious and expectant look on her face.

"Why haven't you ever been married?" he asked finally, deciding to go for broke.

"Wow. Didn't see that one coming." Her feigned look of surprise made it clear she'd seen it a mile away.

Just that fast, however, she sobered. "Okay. The truth is, I came close. Well, at least I thought I was close. Turned out he wasn't close at all."

She fiddled with the sling supporting her wrist, and he had more thoughts of murder and mayhem when he saw the pain in her eyes.

"Only, he never made that little difference in life plans known to me. I still might not know if I hadn't caught him—" She paused, shot him a brittle smile.

"Well, if I hadn't *caught* him. In the interest of keeping this conversation civil, let's just leave it at that."

Bastard, Mac thought. So the guy had led her on, gotten her pregnant, then cheated on her. And Mac had the horrible feeling there might be more to this story than she was letting on.

"He's not only a jerk, he's a fool," Mac said. "I'm sorry. Really sorry he did that to you."

She raised a shoulder, as if it was no big deal, but he saw the hurt and something that even looked like shame in her eyes before she looked away. And, for making her feel that way about herself, Mac hated the guy even more.

"Yeah, well. It's all behind me now."

The plasma screen was on in the background. Times Square was packed as New Year's Rockin' Eve gave a minute-by-minute countdown to the stroke of midnight.

"Hey," she said, her attention suddenly caught by the music. "Remember that band? Oh, my gosh. I love that song."

Mac leaned over and snagged the remote, punching up the volume a couple notches. "Oh, man. I used to make out to that song with Wynona Gray."

She pushed out a laugh. "You used to make out to that song with everyone."

"Just the everyones who wore skirts," he corrected her, then on impulse stood and held out his hand. "Come on. Let's dance out the old year."

If there was hesitation on her part, it was as brief as her surprise. She laughed and took his hand. "Why not."

Oh, he could tell her why not, Mac realized the minute he pulled her into his arms.

Mistake.

Big, big mistake, he thought, liking far too much the way her heat nestled next to his. Hell. She wasn't even aware of what she was doing to him. But she'd know soon enough if he didn't do some serious maneuvering.

"We're going to take you to Times Square now, folks," the TV announcer said as the network cut away from the inside party and scanned the crowd gathered in the street. "The countdown to the new year is about to begin."

They stopped dancing and turned to watch the scene on the screen where the crystal ball had started to descend.

"Ten, nine, eight…"

Mac felt Shallie lean into him a little.

"Five, four, three…"

He turned away from the TV to look down at her…and realized she was looking up at him.

"Two, one! Happy New Year!"

A riot of noise erupted from the television as they stood in the suddenly close silence of his living room, eyes locked, smiles tentative.

"Happy New Year, Mac," she whispered.

"Happy New Year, Shall," Mac said just as softly, and knew, without a doubt that he absolutely should not kiss her.

But it was New Year's Eve.

It was tradition to kiss the one you were with at the stroke of midnight.

And he was just plain nuts. Because he lowered his head. Touched his mouth to hers and realized he wasn't really surprised that she'd lifted her face up to meet him.

It was soft, that kiss. It was sweet. And it was infused with a wary and tentative awareness. Awareness of the heat. Awareness of the little sparks of electricity arcing between them.

Awareness that they both knew what they were doing this time and where it could lead if they dared take it a little farther.

And oddly, Mac sensed the rightness of it all. In the gentleness in which their lips met. In the honesty of affection that passed between them.

The surprise came after. After he had slowly pulled away. After he'd searched her deep-brown eyes and had finally seen what all this awareness between them was really about.

It was one of those "it all became crystal clear" moments. One of those, "why hadn't he seen this before?" revelations.

What was going on here—it wasn't all about attraction. It wasn't all about need—although both were heavily seeded into the mix.

It was about being alone in the middle of a cold winter night when it appeared that the rest of the world was made of couples. It was about being lonely when both of them did their damnedest to never let that show.

Yeah, he realized as he lifted his hand and gently cupped her cheek. Both of them. He was lonely, too…only, he'd never really realized it until now.

For Shallie he suspected it was also more. It was about being afraid. His Shallie was afraid. Afraid of her future. Afraid of the mistakes of her past. Afraid that what she had now was all there was. And she was afraid she would accept and adjust and miss out on something special because of it.

He saw all of that in her eyes. And he saw it clearly because there wasn't a fear or an emotion that he didn't feel himself.

He was weary of the singles scene. Weary of the shallowness of it all, of the game playing and the sport so many made it. Did he expect to find lasting love? No. Not unless it was with Shallie.

That wasn't going to happen. She was still in pain from another relationship. Another man who had let her down. Left her pregnant and alone.

Alone. Like him. He didn't want to spend the rest of his life alone. And he didn't want mistakes he'd made or mistakes his parents had made to harden him and deprive him of something good.

Here was something good. Something like love. At least on his part. Oh, he knew she didn't love him the same way—not the earth-shattering, can't-live-without-you love. But she loved him just the same.

And he had always loved Shallie.

Would it be so bad, he wondered, to let her know that?

In this moment in time, alone together, could he share that with her? If for no other reason than to prove to her she wasn't alone. That she didn't have to be single in a world full of couples.

He kissed her again. And when she kissed him back, less tentatively now, more giving than guarded as she leaned into him and wrapped her arms around his neck, he knew that he was right on target.

There was power in her give, strength in his take. And there was understanding. Unspoken, unselfish and undeniable.

But most of all…most of all, he realized, there was vulnerability. She was so, so vulnerable.

And the real kicker? So was he—except he'd never realized it until right now.

Maybe he needed to think about this. Really think about whether he was willing to spill his guts and possibly settle for an "I love you but I'm not in love with you" apology.

From the look on her face when he pulled away, she needed some think time, too.

"That way lies trouble," he said with a smile meant to reassure yet make known that they were about to tread a potentially dangerous path if they continued doing what they were doing.

She searched his eyes, finally nodded with a tight, sad smile. "Yeah. That way lies trouble."

He expelled a heavy breath. It wasn't exactly relief he felt that she, too, saw the potential pitfalls if they took this further. It wasn't exactly regret. It was something in between. Enough of something that he knew he really had to think about what was happening here.

He pulled back, tipped her face to his with a finger under her chin. "Okay, then. Once again, we avert disaster."

She smiled, he suspected, because he did. "Once again."

He squeezed her arm. "Go to bed, short-stack. We might actually need to talk about this in the morning."

She nodded, turned to leave, then stopped and, stretching up on her toes, kissed his cheek. Her fingertips trailed across his jaw as she left him.

Six

Morning came. And they didn't talk about it. *It* being what they'd both wanted to do last night. *It* being the fact that they'd both spent restless nights alone in their respective beds thinking about *it*.

Seems they were both big talkers after the sun went down and took a day's worth of inhibitions with it, Shallie thought as she sat in the front seat of Mac's truck as they headed down the highway toward Sundown. But in broad daylight, with a sleepless night behind them and the uncertainty of their relationship looming between them, it was easier not to talk about it at all.

Lord knows, they'd both done enough thinking about it. At least she had.

Mostly what she was thinking was, thank God Mac was the man he was or she might have made the biggest mistake of her life last night. Considering some of the mistakes she'd already made, that was saying something.

She didn't want to lose him. Not her friend. And friends and lovers…well, sooner or later you lost one or the other or both. He must have considered the same outcome because, like her, he didn't bring *it* up.

Instead when they'd gotten up, he'd asked her if she'd like to take a trip to Sundown, check out the cabin and if she liked it, move in.

And out of his hair, she thought as the miles flew by. Yeah. Maybe it was time she got out of his hair and out from under foot. She could use the distance, too. To figure out what she was going to do next. And what exactly she was feeling for Mac.

So, to keep their feelings firmly in check, they talked about the size of the snowdrifts along the highway. About the antelope bounding across the fields beside them. They talked about her broken wrist and about the plans he had for the Dusk to Dawn. They talked about anything but last night, like maybe if the subject didn't come up, it had never happened.

The games people play, she thought with a rueful smile.

"And there she is," Mac said as they descended into the valley and turned the final corner that led to town.

Sundown. Sleepy. Serene. Blanketed in white.

A peaceful stillness settled over her. And then she laughed.

"Oh, my gosh. I see progress has hit the great American West. Sundown's gone from a one-horse town

Get FREE BOOKS and a FREE GIFT when you play the...

LAS VEGAS

GAME

Just scratch off the gold box with a coin. Then check below to see the gifts you get!

YES! I have scratched off the gold box. Please send me my **2 FREE BOOKS** and **gift for which I qualify.** I understand that I am under no obligation to purchase any books as explained on the back of this card.

326 SDL EFYD   225 SDL EFW2

FIRST NAME	LAST NAME

ADDRESS

APT.#	CITY

STATE/PROV.	ZIP/POSTAL CODE

(S-D-06/06)

7 7 7	Worth TWO FREE BOOKS plus a BONUS Mystery Gift!
🍒 🍒 🍒	Worth TWO FREE BOOKS!
♣ ♣ ♣	TRY AGAIN!

www.eHarlequin.com

Offer limited to one per household and not valid to current Silhouette Desire® subscribers. All orders subject to approval.

BUSINESS REPLY MAIL

FIRST-CLASS MAIL   PERMIT NO. 717-003   BUFFALO, NY

POSTAGE WILL BE PAID BY ADDRESSEE

SILHOUETTE READER SERVICE
3010 WALDEN AVE
PO BOX 1867
BUFFALO NY 14240-9952

NO POSTAGE
NECESSARY
IF MAILED
IN THE
UNITED STATES

to a one-stoplight town. When did they put the stop-light in?"

"This here ain't no Podunk Hicksville no more, missy," Mac said, launching into his best cowboy geezer voice. "Why, we even got us some o' them whatchacal-lits…some indoor outhouses." He pretended to spit tobacco out the window, wiped his mouth with his sleeve. "Yessiree, Bob. Up and comin'. That's what's happening here."

They were both grinning when he pulled the truck up in front of the Dusk to Dawn. It was a long building in the middle of the block on Main. The white clapboard siding was weathered but the sign above the double glass doors proclaiming it Dusk to Dawn in bold, sham-rock-green letters was crisp and new.

Shallie could see a light on and hear the muffled sound of voices and laughter coming from inside when Mac came around and helped her out of the truck.

"It's open today?"

"Yeah, I decided to open up at noon for anyone who wanted to watch a New Year's Day bowl game."

Judging by the trucks parked outside the bar and res-taurant, several people were doing just that.

"Hold on," Mac said when she couldn't figure out the best way get around the three-foot snowbank the plows had pushed up against the curb. "Here's how we'll handle this."

He picked her up, hefted her in his arms and scaled the drift with his long legs.

"He cooks, he does dishes—and he's got a white knight complex," she said batting her eyes at him when he set her down by the front door. "You're a handy man to have around, macaroon."

He laughed as he tugged open the door. "Macaroon. Haven't heard that in an age or two."

And she hadn't *ever* heard the chorus of, "Welcome home!" that greeted her when he set her down inside.

It had been the exact right thing to do, Mac thought, stepping back and watching Shallie become engulfed in a series of hugs and warm welcomes. After he'd made the call to J.T. a couple days ago suggesting they stage a surprise welcome-home party for Shallie, he'd started having second thoughts. Maybe she was a little too fragile right now. Maybe it would be rushing her.

But as he saw her smile of surprise and unqualified happiness as old friends surrounded her, he was glad he'd gone with his gut instinct. And he was glad he'd put J.T. in charge of contacting all the Sundown locals. J.T. was well liked and persuasive. Looked as if it was going to be a helluva party.

Besides the usual suspects who were always up for a party, J.T. and his wife, Ali, and Cutter and Peg Reno and their two kids, Shelby and little Dawson, were here. Among many others, Lee and Ellie Savage had driven in from Shiloh ranch to join the festivities. Crystal and Sam Perkins and their brood were here, too. Even old Snake Gibson, Joe Gilman and the Griener twins had shown up with their wives and kids.

Mac slipped behind the bar to help his manager, Colt Smith, mix another batch of punch for the kids and tap a keg for the adults who wanted something a little more celebratory to commemorate not only Shallie's return but the first day of the New Year.

"You are a sneaky snake," Shallie accused him an hour or so later as she wandered happily up to the bar and plopped on a stool.

"Guilty as charged." He slid a glass of punch across the bar to her as a whoop went up from across the room when someone's favorite team made a touchdown.

"You never said a word." She smiled over the top of her glass.

It was a good smile. A great smile. A smile that said she was happy as hell.

He wiped a bar rag over the worn and scarred oak surface, set a bowl of peanuts in front of her. "Wouldn't have been much of a surprise party if I had."

It had been fun watching her get reacquainted with her friends, Mac thought. But when her head went down—right after he swore he saw a tear, panic hit him like a brick.

"What? What's wrong?"

She shook her head and when she met his eyes again she was smiling and wiping tears at the same time. "This is the…the nicest thing anyone has ever done for me."

Relief was as sweet as the joy in her eyes.

"Thanks, Mac. I mean…really. Thanks for this. It's great."

While he was moved by her words, it was the look on her face that really got to him. He wanted to vault over the bar, gather up in his arms and tell her that if this was the nicest thing anyone had ever done for her, she'd been hanging with the wrong people.

And he might have done just that if J.T. hadn't shown up right then.

"I've been going to tell you that I know a good lawyer," J.T. said with an ornery grin as he slung an arm over Shallie's shoulders. "I figure you could take this no-count busboy to court and end up with everything but his shirt for breaking your arm. Probably get the shirt, too, if you wanted it, but ugly as it is, I'd take a pass."

"Hey, hey," Mac said affecting a wounded look, "don't be giving her any ideas. And you're in a helluva position to be insulting my taste in clothes. Although, now that Ali is picking yours out for you, there has been improvement."

"Just give me a beer, McDonald. I can do without the lip."

"*You* can do without the lip? See what I have to put up with?" Mac appealed to Shallie, who was grinning at the good-natured banter. "And in my own place."

"Yeah, well, you're just lucky we're a tolerant bunch of folks," J.T. continued, accepting his beer with a nod of thanks, "or we'd have run you out of town by now. Come on, Shall. They're about to crank up the karaoke machine."

"I don't care if you drink in here Tyler, but for God's sake, please don't sing."

"You ever see anyone so jealous of natural talent?" J.T. asked over his shoulder as he herded a giggling Shallie toward the stage.

God, it was good to see her smiling so much, Mac thought, resting both hands on the bar as he watched them walk away. Reminded him of when she was a girl and he and J.T. used to talk smack to each other just to make her laugh.

Hadn't seen all that much of her smile since she'd shown up a few days ago, Mac realized, grinning when J.T. dragged her reluctantly up onstage and shoved a mike in her hand to the enthusiastic cheers of the crowd.

No. He hadn't seen her smile all that much. At least not this kind of smile. Spontaneous, not forced. Truly happy, not an attempt to make him think she was happy. He was damn glad he'd had a hand in making her smile today.

And he'd decided he was also glad he'd put a skid on things between them last night and suggested she move into the cabin today. He'd had a moment of weakness. So had she. She was allowed; he wasn't.

She was pregnant, on her own and about as vulnerable as a body could be. She didn't need him sniffing around, putting on the moves and complicating her life even more.

She needed him to be solid and steady and supportive. End of story.

It was going to be hard, though, he thought as he watched her gamely sing along to an old Dolly Parton song. Her cheeks were flushed with embarrassment; her gaze sought him out in a "help me" plea. She looked so happy and so pretty it did all sorts of weird things to his heartbeat.

He made himself grin and gave her a thumb's-up. Then he went back to the kitchen where he could get a firmer grip on his equilibrium and left her in J.T.'s capable hands.

* * *

It was close to five and almost dark by the time Mac pulled his truck up in front of the weathered log cabin in the woods south of Sundown.

"Stay put," he ordered, jumping out from behind the wheel.

When he rounded the truck and opened her door, Shallie understood why. The snow was knee-deep. Only because his truck had four-wheel drive had they made it up the long lane after they'd left the main road.

"You're going to hurt your back hauling me around," she protested as he hefted her into his arms and carried her up the snow-laden steps to the front door.

"I expect insults from J.T. but not from you—not after I threw you a surprise party," he said, grinning.

"How was that an insult?"

"You obviously underestimate my virile manhood if you think that a lightweight like you could—oh. Ouch. Did I say lightweight? How much did you eat today, anyway?"

She cuffed him on the shoulder. "Okay. Okay. Point taken. I won't insult your supermacho ego, and you won't insult my new and piglike eating habits."

"There you go. Key's in my breast pocket," he said with a nod of his chin. "Fish it out, would ya?"

"Or you could just put me down now."

"I could, but the snow on the porch is ankle-deep so all this show of strength would have been for nothing. Now get the key, woman, and let's get out of the cold."

With a shake of her head, Shallie tugged off her glove and dug into his jacket pocket until she came up with the key. He angled her close to the door so she could slip it in the lock.

"Success," he said brightly, then shouldered open the door and deposited her on a bright, woven rug in the small entryway.

"Oh, Mac," she said when he'd flipped on a light switch. "This is charming."

"Okay, we're going to have that semantics problem again, I see. It's supposed to be rustic."

"Charming. Rustic. Whatever. Don't worry your tender sensibilities. It's very masculine. And very homey. I love it."

The cabin wasn't nearly as large as his new house in Bozeman but it was everything a mountain cabin should be. Lots of warm, aged pine covered the walls of a great room that was living room, dining and kitchen all rolled into one. The tall peaked ceiling was crisscrossed with open beams of aged, native pine and hosted a loft at the far end with yet more natural pine railing. A massive stone fireplace commanded the center of the north wall, the fire well deep enough and tall enough to roast half a beef if need be. A wide, four-shelf bookcase loaded with paperbacks, CDs and DVDs filled the wall space between the living and the kitchen area.

"I know people who would kill to spend a single night in a place like this," she said, spotting more and more touches around the cabin that charmed her. Like the ancient webbed snowshoes crisscrossed above a mantel laden with thick, chunky candles. On the brick hearth sat an ornate iron fire-screen molded in the shape of a bear. Comfy mission oak furniture with cushions covered in Native American prints and colors flanked the fireplace.

Outside the cabin was a world of deep greens and winter whites and darkening sky as snow swirled, weighed down pine bows and drifted onto the corners of the multipaned windows. Inside, woven rugs in pallets of reds and blues and greens warmed the great room while Mac struck a match to a fire already laid out in the hearth.

The dry tinder caught quickly, and soon the licking flames of a toasty fire crackled to life, scenting the cabin of pine tinged with the pleasant aroma of wood smoke.

"Not that Sundown or even Bozeman are hubs of urban activity," Shallie said, forgoing a comfy-looking mission oak sofa and rocker to ease down on a soft rug in front of the fire so she could feel the warmth of it heat her cheeks, "but doesn't it feel a little like we passed through a time warp when we closed the cabin door behind us? I mean—I can almost get a feel for what it was like a hundred or so years ago."

"And what's your interpretation of how it felt?" he asked, walking over to a wall and turning up a thermostat that had obviously been set just warm enough to keep water pipes from freezing.

She raised both shoulders, held her hands out to the fire. "Isolated but cozy. Exciting and a little scary. And on a night like this…romantic," she said.

The minute that thought popped out, she wished she could snatch it back. *Romantic* was not a good thought to express at the moment. Not with the two of them alone again and all those unsettled feelings held over from last night.

And definitely not with her still trying to deal with the way it felt to be held in his arms when he'd carried her to the cabin. He made her feel small and feminine. Protected and cared for. And it made her ache—more than a little—to be held by him again, as he'd held her in his arms last night and kissed her.

She was swamped by a heavy wave of confusion. She didn't want to think of Mac in those terms. She had no business thinking of him that way. And yet…and yet he'd kissed her. Twice. How could she not think about it?

"Yeah," he said, snapping her out of her thoughts, "the prospect of ducking out of the cabin in the middle of a night like this to use the facility that, in those days, would have been twenty or so yards from the cabin, does have a romantic ring to it."

She turned to smile at him. Good thing one of them had things in perspective. Romance clearly wasn't on his mind. His next statement cinched it.

"But then, the prospect of hustling out in the cold again in the morning to hunt us up a possum for break-fast, now, that conjures all kinds of romantic thoughts."

She laughed. "Okay. So I may have glossed over a few of the hardships," she conceded. "Still, you have to admit, this place does take you back in time."

"Yeah," he finally agreed. "It's pretty cool. But speaking of possum," he snagged his jacket, "I'd better get those groceries out of the truck before they freeze or I *will* be hunting up our breakfast in the morning."

When he went outside Shallie rose and explored the

rest of the cabin. Besides the great room and the kitchen, there were two roomy bedrooms with a shared bath between them on the main level. Upstairs, in the loft, was a small sitting area and an open bedroom.

She heard the door open, then Mac's voice boom up the stairs. "Where'd you go?"

"I'm up here."

She started back down the stairs as Mac kicked the door shut behind him, stomped the snow off his shoes, then headed for the kitchen area with his arms full of groceries.

To the fire scents, he added the smell of winter— cool, crisp air and night. It clung to his jacket as she joined him and dug, one-handed, into a sack to help him put the groceries away.

It all felt very homey and domestic. As well as cozy and warm and…right. Just like it felt right to be standing beside him and feeling a warm and encompassing glow.

"Are you planning on feeding a football team?"

"A woman who's eating for two," he said, reaching behind her to open the refrigerator door and stow a carton of milk. "Can't have you going hungry just in case we get stranded out here."

She glanced out the window over the sink where the snow was still swirling. "You think that's a possibility?"

"Not in the next week or so. What you see moving around out there is the wind blowing snow off the trees— but you never know, so I wanted you to be well stocked."

He shoved a dozen eggs and some lunch meat into the fridge. "Before I leave for Bozeman tomorrow I'll put the blade on the truck and clear the lane. There's a four-wheel-drive Jeep in the garage you can use when you want to go into town. It's an automatic so you shouldn't have any trouble driving it."

She felt the tears before she even knew she was going to cry. They just welled up out of nowhere. And so fast, she couldn't hide them.

"Hey. Hey," Mac said so softly when he realized what was going on that it made her cry harder. "What's this? What's wrong? Is it your wrist? Are you hurting?"

Horrified by her outburst, she shook her head, then looked away from him, trying to hide her embarrassment over the sudden attack of waterworks. He wasn't having it.

"Come 'ere," he said gently and, tucking her under his broad shoulder, walked her into the living area and sat her down with him on the sofa. "Tell Daddy all about it."

She pushed out a weak laugh, then sniffed and buried her face in his neck. He still smelled of winter and a little like the Dusk to Dawn and a lot like Mac. Subtly spicy, warm male heat, comfort and strength.

"Come on," he coaxed when she couldn't find the words to express what she was feeling. He cupped her head in his big hand, lightly tapped a finger. "What's going on in there?"

And the dam broke. One moment she couldn't articulate a thing, the next, she was spilling out her feelings like water spilling over a broken dike.

"How did I get myself in this fix? How did I get to the point where I have to rely on the generosity of friends to feed me, to put a roof over my head? To shore up my bruised and battered ego by throwing me a party to take my mind off the fact that I'm without income, without prospects and without a father for this poor little child who never asked to be born to a woman who doesn't have the good sense to take care of herself?"

She stopped long enough to wipe her nose with the tissue he handed her. "I hate it. I hate taking advantage of you. I hate blubbering like a sissy every time my hormones get a little out of whack. I hate lying to Peg and J.T.—at least lying by omission—and not telling them about the baby. I hate thinking that all my life I was ashamed of my mother for relying on cheap men to make her happy, for not loving me enough to make her happy, for…for making such awful judgments in her life. And now…here I am. I'm just like her."

"You are nothing like your mother," he said, her white knight defending her honor. "You're kind and you're smart and I've already seen that you want and love this baby. And you'll love and care for your child. That's something your mother never did for you."

She sniffed again, snuggled closer into the sheltering warmth he offered and felt more hot tears track down her cheeks. "Why couldn't she love me, Mac? What was wrong with me that made it so hard for her to love me?"

His strong arms wrapped her even tighter. "Nothing was wrong with you. Nothing *is* wrong with you. Nothing, you got that?" he added adamantly. "The problem was with her.

"Who knows," he added after a moment. "Who knows what happens to some people to make them the way they are. Maybe she was abused when she was a kid. Maybe she was giving you the best she knew how to give. I don't know," he said quietly. "I don't know what made her tick. But I do know about you. I know what you're made of, short-stack. I knew it the first time I saw you standing up to the Griener boys."

She sniffed again, tipped her head back so she could see his face. "The Griener boys?"

He smiled, all sleepy and slow. "You don't remember?"

"I remember attempting to neuter one of them with my knee."

"I know. I saw it. And I was in awe."

His exaggerated, awestruck look made her grin. "You were afraid you were next, is more like it."

"That, too," he confessed, "but more than that, I saw someone who knew how to take care of herself. And I saw someone I admired. I still see someone I admire," he added before she could make a case for him thinking otherwise.

"You get up, Shallie," he said, tucking her head under his chin. "You take a hit and you get up. You always have. You always will. That's a lot to admire in a person. And that's one of the things I admire about you."

She didn't see much to admire. She saw a lot of mistakes, and they felt too heavy on her shoulders to move her out from under the sense of failure that had settled in for the night.

"You're tired," he said. "You've had a big day. Lots of emotions flowing, right?"

She sniffed. "Stop being so nice to me. I'll just get all blubbery again." She sat up and wiped her eyes. "God. I *hate* this. And don't look at me. I'm a mess."

"So's my shirt," he said, tugging the wet cloth away from his shoulder with such an exaggerated frown he made her laugh. Which, of course, is what he wanted her to do.

"Thanks," she said.

"For being a friend? Hey, you'd do the same for me."

"I don't know," she said, finally mustering up enough spunk to feel a little ornery, "if you threw a hissy fit like that, I'd probably tell you to take a pill."

"See, there's that respect thing again," he groused, even though his grin said he was glad to see her rallying. "I don't get any from J.T., and now I'm not getting any from you."

Shallie woke to the sound of silence. The sunshine slanting in through the cabin window was so brilliant and bright it was almost blinding. The plump down comforter covering her was warm and cocooning. She felt as if she was lying in a nest of feathers, all soft and snug and sheltering. And if it weren't for the demands of her bladder, she'd simply lie there for, oh, another decade or two, and wallow in all this homespun comfort.

The cabin was empty when she tiptoed out of the bathroom a few minutes later. She smelled coffee and followed her nose to the kitchen where, typical of Mac, he'd set food out for her. Chocolate-covered donuts, chocolate iced éclairs, and according to the note he'd set on the counter beside them, there was also tiramisu in the fridge.

She felt a smile crawl across her face. "That man would see me as plump as a Christmas goose if I'm not careful."

It was cute the way he coddled her. Took care of her. Made certain she had her daily chocolate hits. And if she wasn't careful in that area, she told herself as she filled a mug with coffee and wandered toward the big window in the living area that overlooked the forest, all this TLC could become addictive.

In particular, all this TLC from a *man* could become a habit. She'd never had a father to turn to while growing up. Jared had been her only steady relationship, and even before he'd gotten violent, he hadn't been the attentive or coddling kind. In fact, she realized now as she caught a glimpse of Mac behind the wheel of his big black truck, pushing snow with a blade attached to the front of the vehicle, Jared hadn't contributed much of anything in the TLC department. He'd been silent and stoic and, well, she could see now, he'd been a user.

Hmm. Funny how time and distance could add a little perspective. Too bad she hadn't had this kind of perspective when she'd gone "looking for love in all the wrong places" that night three months ago, she thought with a heavy sigh. She wouldn't be in this fix— depending on Mac. Living a lie.

She took a sip of her coffee; Mac made the best coffee.

As she watched him through the window, a fresh wave of guilt swamped her. She should tell him about the baby's conception.

She should tell him.

He looked up from his work about then, spotted her watching him and shot her a big sexy grin and a wave.

She waved back, and that wave of guilt gained weight and settled like a five-hundred-pound monkey on her back.

Yeah. She should tell him. But she just couldn't bear to see the look on his face when he found out the truth. At the moment he was the only stable, caring element in her life. In the short span of a few days, he had become everything to her. Provider. Friend. Family.

She'd always considered herself a strong person. She'd survived a childhood without a father, without the love of her mother. From the time she could remember, she felt as if she'd been on her own.

And now here was Mac. And now she couldn't imagine getting through this point in her life without him.

So no, she wouldn't tell him, because right now, this moment in time, as guilty as it made her feel, she needed him. Needed what he gave her. And of all the things he provided—food, shelter, transportation—it was his friendship, his unbridled affection for her that she needed most.

If she told him, she'd lose him.

"Oh, by the way this baby's father didn't leave me, like you think. No, this baby's father is a married man. Yeah. That's right. I slept with a married man. A man who has children of his own who need their daddy, rat-bastard that he is. He doesn't even know about the baby. He'll never know. At least, he wouldn't find out from me because he doesn't deserve to know."

And because I will not be responsible for breaking up a family, she vowed firmly. It was a little late to think about those particular consequences of her stupidity, but on that count she would not budge.

Mac waved at her again and shot her another big, goofy grin.

No. She would not tell him. Because she would not, could not, lose him.

Seven

"Shouldn't you be wearing your sling?" Mac came in from shoveling and pushing snow to find Shallie dressed and putting the finishing touches on toasted cheese sandwiches and tomato soup.

She was wearing a pair of worn jeans and a pretty pink sweater that made her cheeks look pink, too.

"Doctor said to use my own judgment. And right now it's in my way."

"You didn't have to do this," he said, slipping out of his vest and hanging it on a coat hook by the kitchen door.

"But I wanted to," she said with a smile. "A hardworking man's got to have something warm to eat when he comes in from the cold."

"Hardworking? I'll let you in on a little secret. Any

time I get to play with something with that much horse-power, I'm literally playing, not working."

"Boys and their power tools," she said with an exag-gerated indulgent look.

He made a grunting, he-man sound and beat on his chest. "Me love horsepower and snow blades."

She laughed. He loved the sound.

"All right, tool man, take time out from the macho stuff and refuel, will ya? Eat while everything's hot."

"You shouldn't have any trouble getting out of the lane and into town now," he said, washing his hands at the sink. "I pushed snow all the way to the road, and the weather forecast calls for clear skies and light winds the next few days so there shouldn't be any drifting."

"I can't imagine that I'll need to go anywhere. There's enough food to last for a month, you've got a library that would take a speed reader a decade to plow through and enough movies to start a rental business. Besides. This cabin is like something out of a fairy tale. I don't think I ever want to leave it."

"Just the same, I'll feel better knowing that you can get out if you need or want to. Um. Good," he added, sitting down at the table and digging into his lunch.

"So, you're heading back to Bozeman?" she asked, oh, so casually as she sat down across from him at the small table.

Mac wasn't certain if he heard a little disappointment in her question. Wasn't certain if he was glad or con-cerned that she might miss him.

"Yeah," he said, "I need to get back to the restaurant.

I promised Cara a few days off this week, and I'll need to cover for her."

Then something else occurred to him. Maybe it wasn't the prospect of missing him that made her seem a little reluctant to see him go. "Hey, short-stack. In spite of all this talk of loving the cabin, are you worried about being out here all by yourself?"

"Absolutely not. And I do love the cabin."

"So, you're going to be okay on your own?"

"Mac. I've been on my own for a long time now. I'll be fine."

She'd been on her own too long, Mac thought when he left her an hour later as he drove down the highway toward Bozeman. Maybe that's why it had been hard for him to leave her there.

Maybe that's why he kept thinking about turning around, telling her to repack her bag and come back to Bozeman with him.

The truth was, he was going to miss her like hell. How could that be? Until last week he hadn't seen her for ten years. How could you miss someone who hadn't even been in your life for a decade?

How? Because he'd loved her all that time, that's how. And he'd missed her all that time, too.

He thought about her way too much during the next few days. Called her several times a day because he wanted to make sure she was doing okay.

And because he wondered what she was doing. If she was curled up with her nose in a book or doing something homey around the cabin.

He thought about how quiet his new house seemed

when he came home after a day at SW—which didn't
make a lick of sense because he'd lived alone for almost
ten years now, if you didn't count his college days when
he'd lived first in a dorm, then in a frat house.

It wasn't as if he'd ever had a woman live with him,
yet all of a sudden he missed the softness one could
bring to a room. And the scent. Shallie definitely had a
scent. In the middle of winter she smelled like spring
flowers. Funny, he thought as he checked with his chef
over the evening's specials. Funny how he thought of
that now. With marinara sauce bubbling on the stove and
garlic bread baking in the oven, he thought of spring
flowers and Shallie.

"Phone call, Mac," his bookkeeper said, poking her
head out of the office.

"Who is it?"

"Don't know. She's got a nice voice, though," she
said with a grin.

His spirits dropped when it was a salesperson on the
other end of the line instead of Shallie.

And it was then he decided he'd had enough of
missing her. He was wired for sound when he pulled
into the drive at the cabin and saw Shallie bundled up
in her jacket and waving at him from the front porch.

It had been four days since he'd left her there. Since
he'd scooped out the lane, shoveled the porch and left
her with orders to call him if she needed anything. He'd
also left J.T.'s and Peg's phone numbers with her in case
she needed someone close and in a hurry.

Well, he'd come in a hurry—whether she needed
him or not. And he'd be damned if he knew exactly what
he had in mind now that he was here.

* * *

"What do you think?" Shallie asked, surveying her handiwork. Well, technically, it was her idea but Mac's work.

"I like it," he said, studying the new furniture arrangement with a critical eye. "Should have been this way all along. And I like that wreath over the mantel, too. What I don't like is thinking about how you managed to get it up there."

"No ladders involved, I promise," she said, plopping down on the sofa that now faced the fire and the TV, which sat on a stand to the left of the hearth. "I got it down with a hoe I found in the shed. Then I propped it on the mantel and used the hoe again to lift it from there and slid it on the hook."

"Very resourceful," Mac said, sitting down beside her. "Now hand over that popcorn."

It was funny, Shallie thought as they sat there and one of the DVDs began to play. He'd been gone four days.

She'd thought she would enjoy the solitude. And she had, but she'd also found herself waiting for the phone to ring, knowing when it did that it would be Mac. And it had rung. Often. And they would talk—sometimes for an hour or more. She couldn't remember now what they'd found to talk about. Nothing, mostly. But they'd laughed a lot and he'd fussed over whether she was taking care of herself, and she'd taken great pleasure in telling him that yes, she was being a good girl.

Silly banter. Necessary contact.

And now the contact was physical.

His thigh brushed hers as they sat side by side. She

tried really hard not to notice how strong that thigh was. How much heat his big body generated or how good he smelled. Just like she tried not to make a big deal of it when their fingers tangled, then dueled in the bowl of popcorn she'd popped for the "pseudo movie theater experience" as she'd told him.

"I can't believe these movies hold up after all these years."

They'd loved *Star Wars* when they were kids. They loved it now. Mostly she loved that Mac was back in Sundown and that he planned to spend the night at the cabin.

Truth was, she loved it a little too much.

Since he'd left her four days ago, she'd had a lot of time to think about that kiss New Year's Eve. A lot of time alone. A lot of time wishing they might have talked about it as they'd planned.

She wondered if he thought about it, too.

Beside her he smelled warm and wintry at the same time. She glanced sideways at him. The fire glow did incredible things to his profile as he slouched back on the sofa, his gaze locked on the TV.

Too much of a good thing. Now Shallie knew what that cliché meant. Mac was too much of everything. Too handsome. Too sexy. And tonight probably too close for comfort, given the haywire state of her hormones, which had chosen tonight to remind her she was a woman, with woman's needs.

She had to back away from that line of thought. She had to keep things on an even keel. So when he lifted his hand to dig into the popcorn bowl, she inched it away from him and prepared to shift into good-ol'-buddy sparring mode.

When he felt blindly around for the bowl, she moved it again until she had set it all the way to her left side. Since he was sitting on her right, it finally dawned on him that something was amiss.

"Hey," he squawked when he finally tore his gaze from the movie and discovered that she'd deliberately moved the popcorn out of his reach. "What's the deal?"

"No deal," she said with a shrug.

"Then give me some popcorn before you find yourself in some trouble."

"You want popcorn? Open your mouth."

He was on to her game but went along with it, anyway. "Bet you can't hit it," he challenged and opened wide.

She laughed and, taking aim, tossed one his way.

"That's the best you got?" he taunted, when she missed.

"I can do this," she insisted and tried again. And missed again, several times.

They were both laughing when he reached for the bowl. "A man could starve while you take potshots. Now gimme some of that popcorn."

"No problem." She pelted him with a handful.

He opened his mouth. Shut it. Narrowed his eyes.

"Okay. Now you've done it," he warned, and with a quick, deft move, managed to swipe the bowl away from her.

"Hey, give that back."

"My pleasure." Digging a big hand into the bowl, he fired a handful and hit her full in the face.

She fell back against the sofa cushions, laughing as popcorn cascaded over her head and shoulders. "I don't believe you did that."

"Believe it. You didn't really think you were going to get the best of me," he said, holding the bowl above his head and out of her reach.

"But I'm incapacitated," she wailed between giggles and plucked popcorn out of her hair. "You're supposed to let me win."

"You obviously have never read the bully's handbook. Now hold still," he said, swinging his leg over her lap, then straddling her with his knees dug into the cushions on either side of her hips. "You're about to get full payback for making me suffer through popcorn deprivation."

She shrieked and held up her cast to ward off the attack—not that it did any good.

He dumped the bowl over her head. Popcorn rained down all over her.

"You are crazy!"

"You started it."

So she had.

And as the room suddenly became very quiet, except for the war of spaceships going on in the background, she realized that Mac had become very quiet, too.

He wasn't laughing anymore, either.

Neither was she.

In fact, she was barely breathing…yet very aware of every breath. His as much as hers.

His chest was broad and hard beneath a thick navy-blue sweater. She could see the rise and fall of it so very close in front of her.

She chanced a glance up to meet his eyes, had to lean her head back on the sofa cushion to make eye contact as he stood on his knees poised over her.

He was watching her with eyes that had gone dark and searching. And testing. And asking the same thing she was thinking.

If he lowered his mouth, would she let him kiss her?

She heard a soft plunk, realized he'd tossed the empty bowl beside them on the sofa. Very slowly he lowered his hands to the cushion on either side of her head.

He searched her face, slowly shook his head. "You are one fine mess, Shallie Malone."

Oh, yeah. She was a mess all right. And not just from the popcorn. Her heart was knocking like an air hammer. Her breath was short and choppy. And if she got any hotter, she was going to have to take off some clothes.

Yikes. The look in his eyes told her he was thinking along the same lines.

"You…you made me this way," she managed on a faint, thready breath.

"Messy?" he asked, his voice whisper soft and spring-water deep.

She swallowed, slowly nodded. Messy. Yeah. And hot. And bothered and, man—

"Guess I'll just have to clean you up, then."

Before she could even gulp, he was doing an improvised pushup, lowering his upper body toward her and—oh, sweet heaven above—nibbling popcorn off her shoulders.

"I...um..."

"Shh. Hold still," he whispered, working his mouth along her collarbone, "this is man's work. I need to concentrate."

"Oh. Oh...okay," was the best she could do as he moved back and forth, his mouth gentle, his breath July hot against her throat, against her jaw...against the corner of her mouth.

"Umm. Salty," he murmured taking his time and licking her bottom lip. "And very, very sweet."

His lips felt incredible as they cruised over her face. She could feel the slight abrasive scrape of a day's growth of beard, smell the subtle scent of his after-shave. And, oh, my, she thought as the touch of his lips on the tender skin behind her earlobe made her shiver, she could very easily lose herself in the overwhelming sensuality of what he was doing to her.

Don't stop, she thought. Please, don't stop this time. To make certain he didn't, she lifted her right arm, buried her fingers in the coarse silk of his hair.

"Shallie." His voice sounded raspy, tightly reined. He closed his eyes. Pressed his forehead to hers. "We might be in a little trouble here again. We definitely should have that talk."

"Don't want to talk," she whispered, and lifted her mouth up to his, chasing it when he pulled away.

"Be sure," he said, more plea than warning, "Be very, very sure this is what you want."

She was sure. She was sure she was lost. So very,

very lost in the promise of his kisses, in the tenderness of his touch. And she trusted him. To make everything be all right between them. To make this one of the best experiences of her life.

"I want," she whispered and pulled him back down to her mouth for a long, hungry kiss.

And it was hunger she felt. Hunger to be held. Hunger to be loved. Hunger to believe that finally, finally, she was with a man—a good man—she could trust to always be honest with her.

Honest with his passion. Honest with his expectations. Honest with his love.

And Mac did love her. Just like she loved him. It was the best kind of love. The kind that came without complications. The kind that came from being friends. And this friend would take special care to make things good. To make things right.

She couldn't even call it surrender when he stood, lifted her in his arms and carried her to his bedroom. And she definitely couldn't call it defeat. What she could call it was wonderful as he laid her down on his big bed and then tugged his sweater up and over his head.

Mac knew he shouldn't be doing this. He knew he should be the one to stop it. And if she said the word, he would. In a heartbeat.

But she hadn't said stop. She'd said go. In the thick, rapid beat of her heart. In the long, burning look in her eyes.

He bent over her, kissed her long and deep. And felt one final tug of conscience.

"You sure you're up for this?"

She closed her eyes. And damned if all of her certainty didn't dissolve into a misty panic. "Am I making a fool of myself?"

Oh, God. "For making love with me?"

She swallowed. "For thinking…for wanting…" She hesitated. Looked away.

"For wanting something more for yourself?" he finished for her.

When she nodded, he cupped her jaw, gently turned her head back so she had to look at him. "Not a fool. You're just a little lonely. Just like me," he admitted, then smiled when he saw the disbelief in her eyes.

"Where's the harm, Shallie? We're both unattached, healthy adults who care deeply about each other. I trust you. You trust me. What could possibly be wrong with making each other feel good?"

"Nothing," she whispered. "Nothing at all."

"So we won't be sorry in the morning?"

All her hesitation had faded. She smiled for him. "I've been sorry for a lot of things in my life. I can't imagine that spending a night with you would be one of them."

He breathed a huge breath of relief. "Friends and lovers. Has a nice ring to it." He reached for the hem of her sweater.

"Who knew," he said when he'd helped her out of her clothes and she lay before him in nothing but a pair of lilac bikini panties. "Who knew my little short-stack was so…well…stacked," he finished, because he knew it would make her smile and because she was even more than he'd imagined beneath her jeans and sweaters.

Soft and full. Feminine and beautiful. He lowered his head, bussed his nose around a velvet-soft nipple.

"Are you sensitive?" he asked, remembering that he'd read a pregnant woman's nipples could be very sensitive and sore.

"A little," she admitted.

"Then you'll tell me if I'm too rough," he said just before he surrounded all that velvety softness with his mouth. He suckled her with special care, laved her budding nipple with his tongue and knew from the way she arched into his mouth that she liked it.

That was good. He liked it, too. Liked the way she tasted. Loved the texture and the heat and the plump fullness of her in his mouth. Loved it so much, his sex knotted tight when she moaned and sighed and urged him with the touch of her hand to the back of his head to take her deeper.

He did it gladly. Beneath his hands she felt like silk. All supple, graceful limbs, and skin as fluid as water, as hot as a winter fire.

Her hips were slim. Her tummy still flat, and while he'd seen her legs a hundred times when they'd been kids in the summer, he'd never touched her. The length of her calf. The inside of her knee. The tender flesh where her thighs joined, and a damp scrap of lilac lace—the only barrier between them.

"Okay?" he whispered against her breast when he slipped his fingers inside her panties and met with damp curls.

"Mmm."

He chuckled. "I'll take that as a yes."

"Mmm." She expelled a deep, restless breath when his finger found her wet and slick and swollen and open for him.

A very sensual woman was one Ms. Shallie Malone, Mac thought as he teased her with long strokes just so he could hear that delicious sigh, just so he could feel that quivering little eddy of shock ripple through her.

She was so special to him, he thought, pulling away from her long enough to shuck his jeans and briefs then skim her panties down her hips.

"Tell me what you like, Shall," he whispered, laving attention on her breast again when he'd lie back down beside her. Her skin burned his where they met, naked and needy for the very first time.

"Everything." She lifted her good arm and touched him, experimentally stroking his chest, the line of his hip, searching for his erection between them. Finding. Caressing. Making him moan. "I like everything you're doing to me."

"Oh, sweet woman. I haven't even got started."

"Seriously?" she asked with such a sober look that he laughed. Until she added, "In my experience, by this point in the process, anything to do with me as something other than a receptacle is pretty much over."

He scowled down at her. He didn't want to think about the guy who had cheated on her. He didn't want to bring him into this bed. But he was there just the same. And all Mac could think was the guy was not only a cheating bastard, he was a *selfish* cheating bastard.

"Well hang on, darlin'," he whispered, working his mouth along the fragile line of her rib cage, stopping to indulge in the delectable little dent of her navel. "Before I'm through with you, we're going to reinvent that process."

"I…um…we are?"

She hiked herself up on her elbows, looked down at him as he eased down the bed and made a comfy place for himself between her thighs.

"You…umm…really?" Her words came out on a quivering sigh when he lowered his mouth to her damp curls and kissed her there.

"Me. Umm. Yeah. Really."

And then he proceeded to really, really take her someplace she'd evidently never been before.

She tasted amazing. She made sounds of stunned wonder. And when she finally decided she could relax and let him have his way with her, she opened for him like a flower, came in his mouth with a shattered cry and collapsed back onto the mattress with a serrated gasp.

He was smiling when he crawled back up the bed and settled carefully over her slack and sated body.

"Well?" He nuzzled her neck, licked the salt of her sweat from her skin.

"I always thought," she said breathlessly as she raised a limp hand and cupped his face, "that *necessity* was the mother of invention. Here it was sex. Who knew?"

He chuckled and kissed her.

"Mac." She broke the kiss, made sure he was looking at her. "Thank you. That was…incredible."

"*You* are incredible," he said and, wedging his knee between her thighs, eased himself inside her giving warmth. "Now let's try for amazing."

It *was* amazing. The way she took him in. The way she gloved him, held him and became for him everything he needed her to be.

Supple strength. Sensual woman.

It touched him, the way she gave. Destroyed him, the way she clung then rode with him to a place they'd never been together.

Eight

This was the part where she should be feeling remorse, Shallie thought as Mac slept beside her. This is the part where she should be thinking, Oh my God. What have I done?

But as this big, gorgeous and sensitive man lay with his head on her breast, his arm slung over her waist and his muscled thigh thrown across hers, all she could do was smile.

Who knew? Who knew sex could be about more than giving? Not that giving to Mac wasn't wonderful, but, oh, wow. Taking was a whole new experience for her. And he made it so easy.

He made it so…amazing.

He made it so good, that for the first time she under-stood what all the fuss was about. Just like she under-

stood she'd been looking for something with Jared that
she was never going to find. He hadn't been capable of
this kind of generosity.

"You're awfully quiet."

Mac's voice, deep and sleepy, roused her from her
thoughts.

"That's because I'm very relaxed."

"Relaxed? Not regretful?"

"No." She lifted her hand and touched his hair. "I'm
not regretful. What about you?"

He hiked himself up on an elbow, smiled down at her
in the pale lamplight. "Does this face look like the face
of a man feeling regret?"

She smiled back, stroked his hair. "Actually, it looks
like the face of a very generous, very sensitive lover."

"We aim to please," he said capturing her hand in his,
then pressing a kiss to her palm.

"You've got great aim there Mr.…what did you say
your name was again?"

He grinned up at her from beneath sinfully thick
lashes. "Lucky. My friends call me Lucky. And what
can I call you?"

"Satisfied," she said on a sigh, then stretched in contentment when he kissed his way down the length of her
arm, lingering at her inner elbow.

She liked this. This peaceful, easy feeling. This
playful sexy banter. But most of all she liked the way
he made her feel.

She especially liked the way she felt right now. She
was tired, sated and, thanks to the tender attention he
was paying to the under side of her arm, which just

happened to be in close proximity to her right breast, she was feeling very achy and anxious again.

"You have a beautiful body, short-stack," he murmured as he kissed a circle around her breast, his lips gentle, his breath warm, his tongue skilled, as he lapped at her nipple and brought it to a tight, aching peak.

"You're pretty gorgeous yourself," she said, running her hand down the lean, ropey muscles of his back.

"You do," he said, lifting his head, "have a problem," biting her gently on the chin, "with semantics."

She laughed when he rolled to his back and brought her with him. "Okay," she conceded as she straddled his lap, "not gorgeous. Handsome. Manly. Muy macho. And...oh," she gasped as he settled her over his heat and eased her down onto him.

"You were saying?" He was doing a little gasping, too, as his big hands grasped her hips and moved her slowly up and down.

"Hmm? Mmm. What?"

She couldn't think for the way he felt so deep inside of her. Could barely catch a breath and he expected her to talk?

Her breasts felt heavy. Her heart felt light. And the ache building low in her belly where they met and parted, met and parted, grew to a want so huge, a yearning so vast, it consumed her. Body. Soul. Spirit.

And if she wasn't careful, she thought moments later as she sprawled exhausted and sweaty and spent on his heaving chest, her heart was also going to take a fall.

But she wasn't going to think about that now. She

wasn't going to think about anything but the moment. This special, magical moment where she could give with total trust, take without inhibition. A moment that was hers.

She'd had too much taken away from her in her life. Nothing was going to take this away.

Mac was just debating about mixing up some pancake batter when Shallie, bundled from chin to shin in his navy-blue terry cloth bathrobe and wearing a pair of his wool socks, came padding into the kitchen.

Love hit him smack in the chest like a bullet. God, he loved this woman. It had taken every ounce of restraint not to tell her exactly that when he took her to bed. But he knew his Shallie. The *L* word would have scared her off.

Hell. It scared him and he was the one who wanted to say it.

"Your thermostat running a little on the cold side this morning?" he asked, leaning a hip against the kitchen counter and grinning at the house-frau picture she made.

Her hands were lost in the sleeves of the robe as she shuffled over to the counter and poured coffee into a mug he'd set out for her. "Seems I slept cuddled up to a furnace last night. I haven't acclimated to the loss of the heat source just yet."

"Hmm. How about I make the transition a little easier?" He walked up to her, wrapped his arms around her and pulled her close. "How's that?"

She nestled her head on his shoulder. "I'd say that's just about perfect."

Feeling more contentment that he figured he should

be feeling, Mac just held her that way for a while. She didn't seem to mind. And when he started to sway back and forth—just a little—she started humming. The next thing you knew, they were doing a little slow dance in place, her in his ratty robe, him in his bare feet and jeans.

And damn, if all didn't seem right with his world.

He needed to make sure, though, that things were truly okay in hers. "So, we're good, right?" He tucked his chin to look down at her.

"I'd say we're pretty damn spectacular," she said looking mighty pleased with herself.

"Yeah," he agreed with a final squeeze. "We are."

So. Everything was good. Everything was fine. They'd both scratched an itch. They'd given and received affection and pleasure. And they weren't going to make a big deal of it in the morning.

But later he planned to make a very big deal of it. Later, when she got used to the idea of him and her together. And during the night, when he wasn't making love to her or sleeping, he thought he'd come up with a way to make palatable for her the idea of the two of them together forever.

"How's that cast-iron stomach of yours doing? You up for some pancakes?"

"Don't you ever get tired of cooking for me?" She took her coffee to the table and sat down.

"I'm in the wrong business if cooking tires me out."

"That's what I mean. You shouldn't have to cook when you're away from the restaurant."

"Unless I want to," he pointed out. "And I want to."

"What can I do?"

"Just sit there and look hungry."

"Ha. I can do that without working up a sweat. Speaking of sweat," she unknotted the belt of his robe. "Thanks for warming me up."

"My pleasure."

And it truly had been. All night long.

They were snuggled up on the sofa later that afternoon, sipping hot chocolate, making stabs at reading, but mostly watching the fire and the falling snow. Mac's back was at one end of the sofa and Shallie's at the other; they'd been playing a hit-and-miss game of footsie beneath an old patchwork quilt when Shallie realized Mac was watching her.

She looked up over her open book. "What?"

His expression was thoughtful, searching. "We should get married."

She considered his statement, decided he was just being silly and went back to her mystery novel. "Sure. Okay. Whatever."

The silence from the other end of the sofa lasted a little too long, prompting her to look up again. Her heart kicked her a couple of good ones when she realized he was still watching her. And that he was serious.

"Think about it," he said as if he *had* been doing a lot of thinking about it. "We're not kids, Shall. We're not looking for storybook, fairy-tale love. We're not foolish enough to think that it even exists. Hell. Look at my parents. They were wild, crazy in love when they got married. Seems that ten years later, neither one of them remembered what the fuss was about. The next ten years they just stuck it out because they were too stubborn to fix it…or too mired in their own misery to do anything about it."

He leaned forward, all earnest eyes and handsome face. "I never knew. Never knew they weren't happy together. Never knew that Mom wanted to travel and Dad refused to go any farther than Bozeman. She wanted excitement. He wanted status quo. They were miserable.

"Anyway, Mom finally left him." He tried to sound casual, but his face had grown hard. "I understood that part. More or less, anyway. But it was how she did it that I'll never be able to forgive."

A sinking sensation swamped Shallie as she waited for him to explain. She had a horrible feeling that she didn't want to hear the rest. She was right.

"She had an affair. Some guy from Bozeman. A married man."

Shallie's heart dropped like a stone.

"How…uh, how are they doing…um, now, I mean, since the divorce?" she finally managed to ask, while his words rattled around in her head: an affair…with a married man…never be able to forgive.

He lifted a shoulder. "Dad's doing okay, I guess. It's been five years now. He more or less buries himself in work, lets the rest of the world go by."

"And your mom?" she asked softly while her heart pounded so loud it almost drowned out her question.

Another shrug. A disinterested look that didn't quite ring true. "No clue. Haven't seen or talked to her since she left him."

"Oh, Mac." Shallie could hear the hurt in his voice.

The disillusion. She ached for him. He'd loved his mother. Adored her. And Carol McDonald had adored her son. It broke her heart to hear they had lost contact.

She suspected that it broke his, too, because he quickly moved on.

"The point is, I've got a ton of friends in the same boat as they were. Either trapped in a marriage they no longer have a stomach for or divorced and looking to make the same mistake all over again."

She shot him a concerned look. "So now you want to join the ranks? Make your own mistake?" she asked, hoping to help him realize he was talking nonsense.

"See, that's the thing. We wouldn't be making the same mistakes they did. We know going in what we are to each other. You're my best friend."

"And you're mine," she agreed, "but—"

"No wait. What better foundation could you build a marriage on? Friendship. Respect. Trust. Most important, trust and honesty. We could make this work.

"Plus we've got this damn hot chemistry going on," he added with a grin. "And the baby. I don't want you raising this baby by yourself. It's not fair to you. It's not fair to little Heathcliff. Or little Gertrude," he added with another soft smile.

She studied his beautiful, sincere face. Yes, there was friendship. Yes, there was respect. And the chemistry was incredible. But trust? She trusted him, absolutely. But that coin didn't flip both ways. She didn't deserve *his* trust. She'd lied to him. And God help her, she would continue to lie to him about the baby's father because she just couldn't bear to see the look in his eyes if he knew the whole truth. Especially now that she knew how he felt about his mother.

"Unless," he said, a deep crease forming between his brows, "are you still in love with him, Shallie?"

Oh, it hurt to see that compassion in his eyes. And while it would have been her out—she could flat out lie to him and tell him that yes, she was in love with the father and he would probably back away—she just couldn't do it.

"No. I'm not in love with him. I don't think I ever was," she realized as she thought about Jared. "I just wanted to be."

"See," he scooted forward, looking unreasonably happy. He wrapped his arms around her raised knees and rested his chin on them, "that's what I mean. We all think we want something that doesn't exist. So why not take advantage of something that does?"

When she continued to frown at him, he let out a deep sigh, smiled. "Think about it, okay? Just think about it."

"Okay. I'll think about it. But you'd better think about it, too, friend of mine. Think about why you want to do this. Ask yourself if any of the reasons have anything to do with what *you* want or if they're all about this white knight thing you've got going on. I don't want you offering yourself up for a lifetime commitment for my sake. Not even for the baby's sake."

"Fair enough," he said after another long, searching look. "I'll give it some more thought—providing you seriously consider it, too."

"Do I have to be serious about it right now?" she felt an almost-panicky need to lighten the tension his suggestion had knotted tight in the room. "'Cause the only thing I'd like to get serious about is a nap."

One corner of his beautiful mouth turned up in a crooked grin. "I could go for a nap. Want some company?"

"Depends."

"On?"

"On whether we're going to take this nap with our clothes on or off."

His eyes flickered with fire. "I vote for off."

"Then it's unanimous," she said, and let him draw her into his arms for a long, hot kiss.

"Who knew we'd be so good at this together?" he said, after they'd done everything but nap.

"Yeah," she murmured on contented sigh, just before she nodded off. "Who knew."

She couldn't quite define the feeling. But she liked it, Shallie thought a few days later while she sat in a corner booth at the Dusk to Dawn watching Mac and J.T. give each other grief.

Maybe it was that sense of belonging she'd been looking for when she'd made the decision to return to Sundown. Maybe it was just being around these wonderful people who had welcomed her back—or in Ali's case, had accepted her as a friend.

She finally felt like she was a part of something. Something solid. Something good—which was a rare and special feeling for her.

"You'd think they would run out of insults after a while," Ali Tyler, J.T.'s wife and Sundown's veterinarian, said with a shake of her head as the guys chomped down burgers and the women shared a basket of fries. "I'll never understand that about men. The closer they are, the more smack they dish out."

"I read somewhere that it's a chromosome thing," Shallie said.

She'd liked Ali the first time she'd met her on New Year's day at her welcome-home party. Her opinion of the pretty blonde hadn't changed. It was a plus that she obviously made J.T. a happy man, but Ali's warm, open friendship didn't hurt, either.

"Really?" Ali gave Shallie a wide-eyed look.

"Well, no," Shallie admitted, "but I figure it's as good an explanation as any—and who knows. Someone might have done a study."

Ali laughed and nibbled on a French fry. "You're probably right. What a pair."

"You should have seen them when they were kids."

"Tell me," Ali begged, leaning over the booth top. "I could use some dirt on that man of mine."

"Oh, no," J.T. said with a waggle of his finger, suddenly tuning into the women's conversation. "Shallie. Remember our pact."

"Pact?" Ali grinned from J.T. to Shallie.

"They made me swear in blood," Shallie said.

Ali gasped. "You didn't."

"'Fraid so," Mac admitted, and winked at Shallie. "We've got enough dirt on each other that not one of us would dare open up that can of worms."

"You were kids," Ali protested. "How bad could it have been?"

J.T. glanced at Mac, who glanced at Shallie, who glanced at J.T. They all burst out laughing. Shallie figured they were thinking of the goat that disappeared from Clement Haskins's ranch and ended up in the town library. Or maybe the beautifully gift-wrapped boxful of horse manure that mysteriously showed up on Principal Cooper's desk. Or any one of a number of harmless, juvenile pranks that no one had ever owned up to but that the three of them were behind.

"I'll get it out of you," Ali promised J.T. with a wicked look.

J.T. made a show of looking worried. "She does have her ways," he admitted. "I may break under the pleasure...I mean *pressure*."

"There are words for men like you," Mac sputtered.

"Yeah," J.T. said, caressing Ali with a very private look. "Happy." Then he leaned over and kissed his wife. "Should we tell them?" he asked, holding her gaze as he pulled away.

She nodded, then turned to Mac with a huge smile. "We're pregnant."

Shallie felt herself stiffen. She quickly recovered and gave them both a huge smile. "That's wonderful! Congratulations. When are you due?"

She heard all the animated and happy chatter as a blur of noise as Ali and J.T. filled them in on all the details. She made herself smile. She knew she was smiling because her face felt as if it was about to crack.

And she was aware of Mac watching her, his eyes filled with understanding and concern.

It should be this way for her, Shallie thought,

nodding her head, concentrating to keep her smile firmly in place. She should be able to announce to the world that she was pregnant, that she was thrilled about the prospect of having a baby to take care of and love and provide for.

But she couldn't. At least, she couldn't enjoy the sharing process the way Ali and J.T. deserved to enjoy it. Their baby would be raised in a warm and loving home. With a mother and a father to adore it and each other.

"You okay?" Mac asked quietly after Ali and J.T. had left for home.

"Sure." She flashed him a bright-eyed grin. "Great news for them, huh? They're so excited."

"Yeah. They are. I'm sorry, Shallie. I know that was hard on you."

"Don't be silly. I'm happy for them. They deserve to be excited."

"So do you," he said, wrapping an arm around her shoulders. "You deserve to be happy, too."

"I am," she insisted, and blinked hard and fast to hold back a waterfall of tears. Lord, she hated the way pregnant hormones messed with her emotions. "I am happy."

He pulled back. Cupped her shoulders between his big hands and gave her a little shake so she'd look up at him. "This guy. Whoever he is. He doesn't deserve your tears. And he doesn't deserve you. Or the baby."

And I don't deserve you, she thought when Mac hugged her again. But she was thankful, so thankful, for having him back in her life.

"I've got to go back to Bozeman tomorrow," he said after a moment. "Why don't you come with me? You need to have your cast checked about now, anyway. While you're there, we could find you an OB doc. And we could go to the courthouse. Pick up a marriage license."

He hadn't let the idea of getting married drop. He wasn't pushy about it. Just sneaky. He'd bring it up at the darnedest times. Like when she was feeling most vulnerable. Like now.

"You're kind of like a dog with a bone, aren't you?"

"Bow-wow."

She shook her head. "Mac." And took his hand. "What J.T. and Ali have…well, it's special. Peg and Cutter have it, too. It's proof, you know, that there is such a thing as over-the-moon in love. When two people have that, it's magical. You deserve that for yourself. You won't get that marrying me."

He looked down at their joined hands, absently rubbed his thumb back and forth across her knuckles. "Do you know the odds of two people finding that kind of connection? Approximately slim and none. Okay. Agreed. Our friends have it. But what that does is pretty much cut the possibility of it happening to either one of us down to nil."

"One of the things I've always loved about you is your optimism," she teased in reference to his gloom-and-doom prediction.

"I *am* an optimist, short-stack. But I'm also a realist. So let's be real here, okay?"

"Do we have to?" In the interest of trying to stall this conversation, she attempted to lighten the mood with a pout.

"Yes. I think we do."

He looked so serious suddenly that she sobered, too.

"Raising a baby on your own is not going to be easy. Sundown's a small town. Yeah. You've got good friends who will stand beside you…but do you really want to subject your little one to the small-town gossip?"

Her heart did a little stutter step. She hadn't wanted to think that far ahead. Most of all, she hadn't wanted to remember how it had been for her growing up. Kids were often unkind. And she'd been on the receiving end of snide remarks about more than her hair and her ragged clothes: "How come you don't have a dad? He get one look at that brillo pad hair of yours and hit the road? How come your momma has so many 'friends' comin' in and out of your house?"

"Shallie…honey?"

She looked up, realized she'd zoned out on Mac.

"I'm sorry," he said. "I didn't mean to hurt you."

"No. No, you didn't. You just said something that really hit home, is all. It just…really hit home."

She searched the face of this man who offered her the chance to save her own child from that kind of torment. Who offered her so much more than she really deserved.

And he looked so sweet. And so kind. And so determined that he had the right answer for both of them.

"You're really sure about this?" she asked, making it clear she was asking him if he was sure he really wanted to marry her and if he was sure he knew what he was giving up.

"Last I knew, life doesn't come with money-back guarantees, Shallie Mae. But I come with a few basic promises. I'll take care of you and the baby. I'll be your friend. I'll always be true. And you'll never have a reason not to trust me."

Trust. There was that word again. He promised that she could trust him. And she knew she could. Just like she knew she should trust him with the total truth surrounding her baby's conception.

Yet every time she screwed up her courage to tell him, something stopped her. Something like panic. Something like shame. Something that was too strong to make her do the one thing she knew was right.

So she said the one thing that made it easier, instead.

"Okay," she said, feeling like she was diving off a high board even though she knew that Mac would be there to catch her. "Let's go get that license."

He squinted, searched her eyes. "For real?"

She pushed out a laugh. "For as real as it gets, Brett McDonald, so you'd better be sure you're up for this."

When he smiled at her that way, she could almost believe he loved her. And when her chest filled with a sweet, aching joy, she could almost believe she loved him. Not just a best-friends-for-life-I'll-always-be-there-for-you kind of love.

The other kind. The kind that Ali and J.T. had. The kind the Peg and Cutter had.

Yeah. She could almost believe it. And if Mac hadn't been right about the odds of that happening being slim to none, she might have believed it. Lord knew, she wanted to.

Nine

"You dog, you!" J.T. railed at Mac a day later, even though he was grinning broadly. "I can't believe you didn't tell me.

"And you." J.T. turned an accusatory glare on Shallie now that he was done scolding Mac. "I'm your friend and you kept this a secret!"

Mac grinned from J.T. to Shallie, who was looking a little shell-shocked by J.T.'s reaction to the news that they were getting married.

The truth was, she'd looked a little dazed ever since they'd cut the deal. And he'd felt a little dazed himself. Okay. A lot dazed.

He had a shot. A real shot at making this work. She didn't love the guy. He'd been bouncing off the walls ever since that night he'd asked her, "Do you still love him, Shall?"

Not only did she not still love the creep, she was pretty certain she never had.

It was all he'd needed to charge full steam ahead. And he had—and done his damnedest to take it easy with her. They'd talked about the reality of getting married several times, and she'd insisted she was happy with her decision. And the closer the big day came, Mac realized he was more than happy. Yeah, the prospect of marrying Shallie made him grin. Made him feel mature. Settled. And it was time.

That's why he'd called J.T. and asked him to meet him and Shallie in Sundown. Since they'd wanted to talk with Ali, too, and she couldn't leave the office today because she was short-handed, they met at her vet practice instead of the Dusk to Dawn.

"I believe the correct response to our announcement is, congratulations," Mac said as, careful of her cast, J.T. wrapped Shallie in a big bear hug.

Ali did the same with Mac. "Congratulations!"

"You have my condolences, sweetheart," J.T. said, dropping a kiss on Shallie's cheek. "And I've got to tell you, I'm a little disappointed in you. I always thought you were so much smarter than to get hooked up with a no-account like this."

"Smartest woman in the world," Mac assured his buddy, who turned to him and extended a hand.

"Congratulations, man," J.T. said, serious now. "Really. This is great. Just damn great. I couldn't be happier for you."

"So, I'm in the market for a best man. Since the pickin's around here are pretty slim, what are you doing a week from Saturday?"

J.T. blinked. "No kidding? That soon?"

"Can't think of a reason to wait," Mac said. And he *couldn't* think of any good reason. Even Shallie seemed to want to make it official as soon as possible. Whether it was for fear that she'd back out or actual excitement, he didn't know.

All he knew was that his plan to play it loose and easy and slow had worked. She hadn't shied. She hadn't spooked. She'd said yes.

And he'd damn near blown a gasket.

She'd said yes. And he was determined that someday in the near future she'd say yes again to another question. One that went something like "Do you love me, Shallie?"

"Well, I'm your man, then," J.T. said, beaming. "Just tell me where and what time."

"Ali?" Shallie turned to her new friend. "I know we haven't known each other for long, but—"

Ali actually squealed. "I would be honored," she said, interrupting Shallie before she'd finished asking her to be matron of honor. "Oh, this is so exciting."

Mac loved the look that crossed Shallie's face when Ali responded with such excitement. He'd known she was hesitant to ask Ali to stand up with her, and on some level he understood the reason why.

He'd never had a doubt that Ali would be thrilled. Shallie had had doubts, though, and he figured it stemmed from the way she'd felt about herself from the time he could remember. Hell, when your own mother didn't want much to do with you, it was a leap of faith to think anyone else would. And Shallie didn't leap toward anything. She picked her way very carefully.

Ali's open and excited reaction was exactly what Shallie needed. It had been a major hurdle for her to let down her defenses enough to trust that someone might actually want to be a part of her life.

Yeah. It had been a major hurdle. And, judging by the look on Shallie's face, she was glad that she'd taken the chance on Ali.

The woman he saw right now was a happy one. And he liked it.

"Have you bought your dress yet?" Ali asked.

"My dress?" A look of minor panic replaced Shallie's smile. "I'm afraid I haven't gotten that far."

"Great. Then we can go shopping together."

God bless Ali Tyler, Mac thought later, as he and Shallie headed for the cabin. The two women had gotten their heads together to plan a shopping trip to Bozeman. Mac and J.T. had shot the breeze, occasionally warned the ladies with the bright eyes and excited smiles not to get too carried away and grinned because Mac knew he'd indulge Shallie in about anything she wanted to do to pull off her idea of the perfect wedding.

Well, not perfect, he realized. They couldn't do perfect in a week. But they could come pretty damn close, he'd decided and had already set the wheels in motion to make sure they threw one of the biggest, fanciest receptions the Dusk to Dawn had ever seen.

"You know," Shallie said, standing by the hearth one night after Mac had rebuilt the fire. "It would have been a lot easier if we'd just driven to Nevada and done this in a civil ceremony."

"Oh, boy. Here we go again. Haven't we had this discussion once or twice already and nixed the idea?"

"You nixed the idea," she pointed out.

"Come 'ere," he said and patted the sofa cushion beside him. "Let me explain this to you one more time."

With a self-conscious smile she eased down beside him, let her head fall back on his shoulder when he draped his arm around her.

"Comfy?"

She nodded and turned into him, snuggling close. He loved that she was so comfortable touching him now. Loved that they were so easy with each other.

"Now listen very carefully. We are not going to Nevada for a quickie civil ceremony. We're going to get married in the company of our good friends, and then we're going to throw the biggest reception Sundown has ever seen. Why? Because a woman deserves to have a special day to remember and tell her children and grandchildren about."

He ran his hand up and down her arm in a slow caress. "And because a man wants to have a memory of his wife all dressed up and pretty for him when he thinks back on that day."

"I hate to break this to you McDonald, but in spite of your big talk to the contrary, you're a romantic, you know that? Even though you claim you don't believe in fairy-tale love."

Yeah. He was a romantic, all right. And someday he'd let her know exactly how romantic he was.

"What I am," he said choosing his words carefully, because for some reason he was suddenly having a hard time picking the right ones, "is a man who cares very much for a certain woman. I want to make you happy, Shall. And I want to start out by giving you a special day."

She tipped her head way back so she could look up at him. Her eyes were a misty, shimmering brown, and they were brimming with something that gave him a little lump, right in the center of his throat, and made it hard to swallow.

"You are such a good man," she whispered, touching his face with her fingertips, touching his heart with her smile.

They made love slow and easy, then. With the fire crackling in the hearth and the sun sinking low in the horizon.

"I'll do right by you, Shallie," he promised, moving in and out of her as she clung and arched and gave herself over to his loving.

"I'll do right by you and the baby."

"I know," she whispered back. "I…know."

When it was over she cried. His tough Shallie who never cried when someone hurt her. He held her close and stroked her hair and told himself it was all about those hormones she was always cussing. He pressed a soft kiss to the top of her head. Bless her, those hormones did give her fits.

She had to tell him, Shallie thought as she lay awake well into the night that night. He was so good.

So kind. And so trusting that she was the person he needed her to be.

She had to tell him. And in the morning she would. Maybe he'd understand. Maybe he'd forgive her.

Like he forgave his mother? she wondered, and snuggled closer to her future husband's side.

It didn't matter. Somehow, some way, she had to screw up the courage to tell him about her one night-stand with a married man.

She cringed, just thinking about it. Even so, even if he saw her for the horrible, deceitful person she was and he changed his mind about marrying her, she couldn't live with herself if she didn't come clean. And she had to do it before the wedding, which was only five days away.

He stirred in his sleep and pulled her closer to his side. And she realized, with a horrible ache in her heart, how much she was going to lose if she lost him.

She was going to lose the best thing that had ever happened to her. She was going to lose the one person who had ever really cared about making her happy. And, surprise, surprise, she *was* happy. Really happy.

With distance from her old life and the physical surroundings of her failures and with Mac's tender support, she was actually more happy than worried about the prospect of being a mother. She'd needed someone to love for so long. Someone to love her. She'd thought it would be just her and her baby. She'd thought she could make it enough.

But now there was Mac. And now she knew he truly did make her life complete.

That was the biggest revelation of all. She'd been determined to classify their relationship as friendship. She'd been determined they were marrying for convenience. For the sake of the child. And because Mac was ready for a family and had given up on love.

Well, guess what? She hadn't. She'd thought she had. She'd thought there wasn't a chance on earth that she'd ever fall in love again.

Turns out she was wrong. Turns out she'd never been in love at all. Not really.

Well, she was now. For the first time.

Mac. She loved him. Loved him for being there for her. Loved him for wanting to take care of her. Loved him for being the kind of man he was.

But most of all, over the course of the past week and a half, she'd fallen in love with him as she'd never loved another man.

It was more than love now. At least, it was more than any love she'd ever known. She couldn't wait to see him every morning. Couldn't imagine going to bed without him at night. Adored it when he touched her, kissed her, made love to her like she was the most special woman in the world. No one had ever given her that before. No one.

Her macaroon. Her white knight.

And because she loved him, she had to tell him in the morning, she reminded herself, sobering in the dark.

But when morning came, he was gone. She found a note tucked under a plate of chocolate-glazed long johns:

Hey, Shall,
You were sleeping so sound I didn't want to wake you. Cara's got a problem with the refrigeration

at SW so I had to head back to Bozeman. I'll call
you later, okay?
XOXOs, Mac.

Shallie slowly folded the note. And felt a relief too big
to be anything but cowardice. She'd been given a reprieve.

And she was grateful.

Tonight, she promised herself, walking over to the
kitchen window to watch a vibrant red cardinal eat
cracked corn from a feeder Mac had put up, for her as
much as for the birds. She would tell him tonight.

But he didn't make it back to Sundown that night.
The refrigeration problem had become a dilemma and
he'd had to drive to Helena for parts.

During the course of the week, a dozen things dis-
rupted their communication flow. Even when Shallie
and Ali spent a day in Bozeman shopping for their
dresses and they stopped into SW for lunch, Shallie
couldn't find the right time to talk to him.

The next thing she knew it was Saturday, their wedding
day, and, for a number of reasons, she still hadn't told him.

More to the point, she'd started to believe there might
be a valid reason that "life" kept interrupting her good
intentions.

Maybe fate was intervening on her behalf. Maybe it
was okay that he didn't know. Maybe it was okay to
leave her past in the past and start this new life with Mac
without the weight of her mistake hanging over them.

And maybe, just maybe, she deserved to have him
think of her the way he wanted to think of her, not the
way he would be forced to think of her if he knew.

Whatever the reason as she slipped into her wedding dress and put the final touches on her makeup, the only thing she was certain she was going to say to Brett McDonald this afternoon, was "I do."

Besides Mac and Shallie, only J.T. and Ali and Mac's dad, Alex, witnessed the vows as Preacher Davis performed the ceremony at the Sundown Congregational Church where they were pronounced man and wife.

The reception, however, was a different story. They wanted *all* of their friends at the reception.

The Dusk to Dawn was packed. From the bar to the eating area to the dance floor, it was party room only.

And for Sundown it was the party of the decade.

"How'd a couple of duds like us rate women like them?" J.T. asked Mac as they stood, beers in hand, watching Ali and Shallie dancing with the Griener twins.

Mac grinned and shook his head. "Beats the hell out of me. Sometimes it's best not to question good luck."

"Amen to that. Hey…there's Lee and Ellie Savage. I've got to go say hello. Be right back."

Mac was barely aware of J.T. leaving. Hadn't been aware of much of anything except Shallie since he'd caught sight of her walking down the aisle toward him at four o'clock this afternoon.

Shallie had always been a looker. She had that wholesome, girl-next-door-with-an-attitude look that had always made him think of a modern-day Annie Oakley. *Grit* was a word that always came to mind when he'd thought of her.

It wasn't the word that came to mind today. A lot of others did, though.

Beautiful, for one.

Special, for another.

Mine, however, topped the list.

As of today, Shallie Malone was Shallie McDonald. And she was his. To take care of. To share with. To have and to hold and to love and to cherish.

He'd meant every word when he'd said them. It wasn't that he hadn't expected their vows to have meaning. He just hadn't expected them to mean so much.

He grinned as Billie Griener twirled Shallie across the dance floor and she threw Mac a look that clearly cried, Help!

Setting his beer on the bar, he set off through the crowd to rescue his very own damsel in distress.

"I'll be taking my wife back now," he said, tapping Billie on the shoulder.

"Yeah, I saw the way you were watching us," Billie teased. "Figured you'd get to worrying 'bout me beating your time."

Mac grinned at Billie's receding hairline and to-bacco-stained teeth and pulled Shallie into his arms. "You read me right, man. Now give me some room to work here so I can make her forget all about you."

With a chuckle, Billie slapped him on the shoulder and headed for the bar.

"So," Mac said, slowing things down to an intimate, easy sway even though the band he'd hired was rocking to a Montgomery Gentry song, "you having a good time?"

"The best." When she looked up at him, her smile was so huge and bright it staggered him. "And even better now. Thanks for the rescue mission. I don't think my feet could have taken one more hit from Billie's boots."

"God, you're pretty," he said because he just couldn't hold it in. She'd done something special with her hair. Nothing too fancy. Nothing too much could be done with those short, springy curls, but she'd tamed them some and tucked a little sprig of flowers above her right ear, and damned if she didn't make him think of some kind of a forest nymph.

There was a little extra pink in her cheeks, a shimmery gloss on her lips—probably the dress had something to do with it, too. He didn't have a clue what it was. Silk maybe. And pale pink with long sleeves that covered the smaller cast the doctor had put on just yesterday. She looked sleek and slim and soft. Felt that way, too.

"You don't look so bad yourself, cowboy."

Just for her, because she'd remarked how sexy J.T. had looked at his and Ali's wedding—Ali had had them for dinner last night, and Shallie had spotted the picture on the wall—Mac had dressed in a black western-cut suit.

"Yeah, well. Told you I cleaned up pretty good."

"That you do," she agreed with the softest smile. The kind of smile that made him feel all full inside.

This was going to work, he told himself as the band changed gears and launched into a ballad. This marriage was going to work. Everything felt right about it.

More right, even, than he'd thought it would. He felt it

more and more every day. And seeing Shallie today, glowing and happy and knowing he was in part responsible for that happiness, he'd started to feel something else.

He could make her fall in love with him. He smiled to himself and lowered his head so he could nuzzle her ear and get a whiff of that amazing scent she was wearing.

Yeah. He could make her fall in love with him. This woman who was the antithesis of almost every woman he'd ever been involved with. A woman who didn't play games. Whose life didn't revolve around how she looked. A woman who wasn't after him for his money and wasn't overly impressed by his success.

She was fun and funny and sincere.

And she didn't have a deceitful bone in her body.

She was just Shallie. Honest. And real. And true. In short, she was perfect.

Any man would be lucky to have her. And as he held her in his arms and she snuggled up against him, he counted himself as one damn lucky man.

"What I'd like to know," Mac murmured as they cuddled under the big quilt on the floor in front of the fireplace later that night, "is what kind of woman prefers winter in an old cabin in the mountains to a condo on Maui for a honeymoon destination?"

Shallie snuggled closer, loving the feel of Mac's big naked body pressed against hers, sharing his heat with her. "I don't need Maui."

"I'm not talking about need. I'm talking about what you want."

"I want what I've got. And it's right here."

"Six-foot snowdrifts, Arctic winds, the possibility of power outages—"

She cut him off with a finger pressed to his lips. He promptly sucked it inside his mouth, gently latched on. "I want a home, Mac," she said, hearing her voice clog with emotion.

He heard it, too. Let go of her finger and looked into her eyes.

"I want a home," she repeated softly. "It's all I've ever wanted. You've given it to me." She searched his beautiful face, cupped his strong, hard jaw in her palm. "What more could a woman want?"

He was quiet for a long moment before he slowly shook his head. "You're one of a kind, short-stack."

"Broke the mold, all right," she agreed, giving him a smile.

"No. I mean it." He kissed her forehead, then her brow, then her cheeks. "I don't know anyone like you. Unassuming. Unspoiled. Honest."

She felt those damn tears well up again. Not just from the tender way he kissed her, not just from the sincerity of his words, but from the guilt over just how dishonest she had been with him.

"Mac," she began, overcome by an urge to blurt out the truth about the baby. Get it off her chest.

He shook his head. "No, wait. I'm not finished. There's something I need to say to you. Something I should have said before today but didn't have the guts."

She swallowed hard, her heart pounding, her nerves shredded as she waited him out. She'd let him have his say. Then she'd tell him.

"You know that notion of love and happily ever after I've been speaking out against?"

Heart in her throat, she nodded.

"Well, the deal is, I didn't know what I was talking about."

Her heart stopped then. Flat-out, still as stone, stopped.

"I want happily ever after with you, Shall. I want love with you. And I'm thinking maybe I'm going to get it."

"Mac—"

"There you go," he scolded, a smile in his voice, "Interrupting me again. I love you, Shallie. I've always loved you. Honest to God, head-over-heels, love you. There. I'm done. Now you can talk."

Like she could talk. Joy rolled over trepidation. Hope won out over guilt. She threw her arms around his neck, clunked him on the back of her head with her cast and made them both laugh. And then she just hung on. To this man. This beautiful, amazing man who thought he loved her.

"Hey. Hey, hey," he soothed. "Are you crying again?"

She laughed, pressing her face against his neck. "How do you think I'm going to react to a statement like that?" she sniffed.

"Oh, I don't know. I was kind of hoping you might tell me how *you* felt about the idea of love and happily ever after and stuff."

She sniffed again. "Stuff, huh?"

"Well, mostly about the love part."

She pulled back so she could look into his beautiful gentle eyes. "I really, really like the love part. In fact, I'm pretty much in love with the love part."

He smiled and her world went one hundred percent right again. "Pretty much?"

She nodded.

"How pretty much?"

And laughed. "Pretty much pretty sure that I pretty much love you, too."

He looked so happy. Not just the usual, good-natured, Mac-the-good-guy happy. But a-man-in-love happy.

"Lots of pretties in there."

"Yeah. Lots."

"So," he said, stroking a hand along her hip beneath the quilt. "This is like a good thing, right?"

"Yeah." She laughed again. "It's like a good thing."

He watched her face for the longest time, then turned serious as he slid his hand around and covered her stomach with his big palm.

It felt warm and gentle and protective against her.

"I want this to be *our* baby, Shallie. I want to raise this baby as mine. Yours and mine."

Her eyes blurred and burned and it felt like her heart was going to push its way out of her body through her throat. "Mac."

His big hand slowly caressed her there, where the baby slept and grew. "Our baby, Shallie. Okay?"

How could she say no to this gift he was giving her child? A gift that should be a birthright. A right she'd never had. How could she deny it to her child?

And how could she tell him the truth now and risk losing it all?

"Okay," she managed to whisper between trembling lips. "That is so very, very okay."

Ten

While the last of the women who had attended her baby shower said their goodbyes, Shallie bounced little six-month-old Jacob Savage on her knee. The baby drooled and grinned and made Shallie's heart swell with anticipation of her own baby's arrival in less than four months.

"He's such a sweetheart," she said to the baby's mother, Ellie Savage.

"He's our little miracle," Ellie agreed, beaming as she helped Peg Lathrop tidy up the Dusk to Dawn which had been closed today for the private shower.

Ali and Shallie started to show about the same time a couple of months ago. Shallie was sure people had wondered about the timing of her pregnancy but they were too kind to say anything. It was about that same time that Peg Reno and Ellie decided it would be a fine time for a joint baby shower.

They'd done it up right, too. Shallie was overwhelmed by the generosity of the Sundown women— some of them she barely knew. Judging from the look on Ali's face as she organized her gifts so J.T. could help her haul them home, Ali was pretty amazed, as well.

They were wonderful people, these new friends of hers. Shallie had gotten to know Lee and Ellie well during the past couple of months since she and Mac had gotten married. During that time, she'd grown to admire the young woman who struggled with epilepsy, yet didn't let it keep her from enjoying life to the fullest. Even if it had meant risking her own health to conceive and deliver this amazing child.

"Your momma thinks you're a miracle, baby boy," Shallie said, lifting Jacob to her shoulder and snuggling him close. "I have to agree. You're such a good baby," she murmured, rubbing his back and inhaling the wonderful scent of baby and powder and thinking that it wouldn't be long now until she held her own baby.

Hers and Mac's. And that's exactly how she thought of the life growing inside of her. Mac's child.

"I think that pretty much covers it," Peg said, looking around at the tidy room.

"You guys are too much," Ali said, her look encompassing both Peg and Ellie.

"Agreed," Shallie chimed in as Ali held her arms out so she could have a turn at cuddling Jacob before everyone headed for home.

"Any excuse for a party," Peg said with a grin just as the front door opened.

"Did someone say party?" J.T. beamed as he walked into the Dusk to Dawn followed by Mac, Cutter Reno and Lee Savage.

"Sorry, guys. It's all over but the heavy lifting." Ellie handed the diaper bag to Lee, then pried Jacob out of Ali's arms so she could bundle him into his little snowsuit.

"And what did you four troublemakers find to do to keep yourself busy for the last few hours?" Peg asked, grabbing her coat.

Cutter hurried over and helped her into it. "Just a friendly little card game."

"Friendly?" Mac snorted. "It was cutthroat."

Lee slapped him on the back and addressed the room in general as J.T. gathered up an armload of baby gifts and winked at Shallie. "Treat him with kid gloves tonight, Shallie. The man had a little string of bad luck."

"Card sharks, is what they are," Mac grumbled.

"Poker face is what he isn't," J.T. pointed out with a nod in Mac's direction. "But he *is* a sore loser."

"Har. Har." Mac walked over to Shallie, sat down in a huff.

"What's the matter, sweetie? Did those mean boys pick on you today?" She patted his hand with staged sympathy while the other guys looked anything but sympathetic.

"They beat me out of my lunch money, Mom," he whined, playing for a laugh—which he got along with a few more jabs from the guys before they all collected their women and headed out the door with a chorus of goodbyes.

"Thought they'd never leave," Mac said, urging her onto his lap. He kissed her. Smiled. "So, did you and Heathcliff rake in lots of loot?"

She laughed. "Me and *Gertrude* did pretty darn good. Wait until you see all this stuff."

"Had a good time, did you?"

She nodded. "Had a great time. These people…well, they're wonderful."

He kissed her again. "So are you. Now, what do you say we get this stuff loaded up and head for home?"

"Sounds good to me. I'm beat. Opening presents is very exhausting."

"Your wrist hurting?"

"No. Oh, no," she said quickly seeing the concern in his eyes. He'd been that way ever since she'd had the cast removed a month ago. "Will you quit worrying about my wrist? It's fine. Perfect. I was kidding, okay? Now, let's start loading up so wc can go home."

"You will load nothing. I'll handle it. I don't want you lifting one thing."

That was another thing about Mac. He was a protector. If he had his way, he'd keep her in a glass cage where nothing could get at her. No germs, no possibility of accidents.

The independent side of her would complain, but he was so cute about it she couldn't bear to burst his bubble.

"Sit tight for a second," he said, sliding her off his lap. "I need to check on some things in the kitchen. Be back in about five minutes, and then I'll load this major haul into the truck."

"I'm not going anywhere," Shallie said, and watched him disappear into the kitchen.

Life, she decided, lifting a little yellow sleeper out of a box, just couldn't get any better. The past two months since they'd gotten married had been the best of her life. Mac was sweet and gentle and so much fun to be with. And he was an inventive and selfless lover. She got a little chill just thinking about the way he made her feel when he made love to her.

Yeah, she thought, holding the little sleeper to her breast. Life just couldn't get any better. For the first time in her life she had a home—a complete home. She had someone who loved her. Her. Just as she was, in the form of a man she still couldn't believe she'd been lucky enough to want to be a part of her life.

Yeah. Life was perfect.

And then the front door opened with a cool rush of mid-March air.

A man's silhouette filled the dark doorway.

"Hello, Shallie." He stepped into the light.

And Shallie felt her perfect world slip out from under her like a sinkhole.

"Jared."

Mac took a little longer than he'd thought, stocking the cooler for the bar action that the Dusk to Dawn was sure to see tonight when they opened back up to the public at six.

He was afraid Shallie might have given up on him when he finally shut the kitchen door behind him and headed for the main room.

"I told you to leave," he heard Shallie say before he saw her and every protective instinct in his body went on red alert.

She was standing and she looked agitated, and whoever was the cause of that agitation was some guy who looked about as determined to stay as she was for him to go.

"Damn it, Shallie, I didn't spend five months hunting you down, then drive two thousand miles to find you, just to turn around and go back to Georgia without you. I made a mistake, all right? I realize that. I said I was sorry. So quit talking nonsense and get in the car."

"I believe the lady said she wanted you to leave." Mac walked up behind Shallie, put his hands on her shoulders and gently set her behind him.

"Mac. It's okay. I can handle this," she said quickly.

The guy glared at Mac. "Who the hell are you?"

He was about Mac's height and weight. His eyes were a mean brown, his attitude superior as hell. And Mac didn't much care for the way his fists were clenched at his side.

He also didn't care for the implications. This had to be the guy. The guy who'd cheated on Shallie and left her pregnant.

Mac's gut clenched as he sized him up. He hated him on sight. Hated to think of this guy touching Shallie. Hated to think of him having anything to do with her. And rumbling through it all was a growing and consuming concern that he might be here to stake some claim on the baby. The baby Mac had come to think of as his own.

"I'm the guy," Mac ground out, "who's going to

invite you real nice-like to do as my wife says and get the hell off my property."

"Wife?" His dark gaze shifted from Mac to Shallie who had moved out from behind Mac and was trying to insinuate herself between them. He grunted, threw her a look of disgust. "Well, it didn't take you long to find another bed to crawl into, did it?"

"One more word," Mac ground out, pushing past Shallie and grabbing the guy's jacket in his fist and twisting, "and I'll kick your ass from here back to Georgia."

"Stop it!" Shallie reached for Mac's arm, tried to push him away. "Please. Stop. Mac. Don't. He's not worth it.

"Jared," she said, turning to the guy as Mac reluctantly let him go. "Leave. Now."

Jared gave a macho shrug of his shoulders, shot Shallie a glare. "This is what you want?" He lifted a hand toward Mac. "You want to be stuck out here in the boonies with cowboy Bob here?"

"Look, you're the one who screwed up, okay?" Mac was pissed now. Royally pissed. He shoved Jared hard in the middle of his chest, knocked him a step backward. "What kind of man makes promises to a woman then cheats on her? What kind of a man walks away from his own baby?"

Jared staggered when Mac shoved him, caught his balance and glared from Mac to Shallie. "Baby? What the hell are you talking about?"

"I'm talking about how you got her pregnant and then walked out on her."

"Whoa. Whoa." Jared lifted his hands beside his head

in a show of supplication. "I don't know anything about a baby. Is that what she told you? That I got her pregnant?"

"Figures you wouldn't own up," Mac said with a snarl.

"Own up? Hell, cowboy," Jared said with a cocky and ugly smile, "I'd own up if it was true, but the fact is, I'm shooting blanks, man."

Mac narrowed his eyes.

"Vasectomy," Jared supplied, looking smug. "Three years ago. I don't want any little bastards running around costing me money."

Mac glanced at Shallie. She'd gone statue still. Ghost white.

She closed her eyes. Swallowed. "You need to leave now, Jared," she said in a voice that sounded hollow and weary and empty of conviction.

Jared looked from Shallie to Mac then smiled a nasty smile. "Looks like maybe I do. My mistake, cowboy," he said, backing toward the door. "She's all yours. Her and the brat."

The silence that rang in the wake of his departure could have filled the Grand Canyon.

Mac was aware of Shallie suffering beside him. Aware but unable to do anything about it.

He felt as if he'd been gutted. He felt as if he'd been strung out, hung out, stripped of everything he thought he knew. About her. About them.

She'd lied. Shallie had lied to him.

It didn't compute. It didn't add up to what he knew about who she was and what she was.

And it left him feeling so fractured and confused he didn't know what to say. How to handle the sense of betrayal, the surge of anger that had him glued to the spot, his gaze stuck on the door that had shut behind the man who had just changed his life forever.

"Mac—"

He held up a hand. Shook his head. "Don't."

"Please." There were tears in her voice. No doubt, in her eyes as well. For once it didn't affect him. He didn't want to hear what she had to say. Didn't want to look at her.

"Let's get these things into the truck," he said, and started stacking boxes and grabbing sacks.

He walked around her where she stood in the middle of the room, looking helpless, looking hopeless.

"It was after I caught Jared cheating," she said and he stopped cold in his tracks. Back stiff. Shoulders back.

"He'd hurt me, you know? And I don't mean just hurt me because he cheated. He, um, he hit me."

All the muscles in Mac's body clenched tight. His gut knotted. And for a second, there, he thought he was going to be sick.

"That was it for me. I left him. And then I wallowed. If you can imagine, now that you've had the pleasure, I actually felt like I'd lost something other than my self-respect. For a month I threw one big pity party. Poor Shallie. Nobody loves me. Nobody wants me."

Mac swallowed. Lowered his head. And still he couldn't turn to her.

"Anyway," she said, sounding weary and resigned, "a couple of the girls I worked with dragged me with them to a bar one night. Just to make me get out. You know. Crawl out of my cave. This…this guy…"

She stopped, her voice trembling.

"This guy," she began again after she'd collected herself, "he was so…nice to me, you know? Made me feel worth something again. He was charming. And he charmed me."

Another pause, as if she was working up the courage to go on.

"Shallie," he finally said, needing to stop her. He didn't want to hear any more.

"It wasn't until the next time I saw him a week later that I found out he was married," she finished with a truckload of guilt weighing down her words.

Married. She'd slept with a married man.

Something inside of him went stone-cold dead.

"I didn't know. I swear I didn't know. And after… after that night, after I found out, he…he kept after me no matter how often and how vehemently I told him no. And when…when I found out I was pregnant. Well. I'm not a home wrecker, Mac. He has a wife. Kids."

"Anyway," she said after the moment it took her to compose herself, "I had to get away from there. And that's why I ended up here."

Mac drew a deep breath, let it out, thought of his mother who had cheated on his dad with a married man. And couldn't find it in himself to sort one situation from another.

"I meant to tell you."

"Then why didn't you?" he asked, finally finding his voice and with it the hard edge of anger.

"I...I tried. I really tried. But it was just so easy to let things get in the way of the truth. You...you made it so easy."

"Ah. So it's my fault."

"No. That's not what I meant. Mac—"

"Look. Let's just get out of here. I don't want to talk about it. I don't want to hear about it. It's over. It's done. Nothing's changed. You're still pregnant. We're still married. Let's just leave it at that."

Even as he said the words, he knew they were lies.

Everything had changed.

Everything.

Winter was almost over, but Shallie had never felt so cold. Cold outside. Cold inside.

A silence the size of a glacier radiated from Mac like an Arctic chill as they rode from Sundown to Bozeman.

She understood. She understood his anger. Understood his disappointment. In her. In who he'd thought she was.

And it was no one's fault but her own. She was the one who'd made the mistakes. She couldn't even blame Jared for showing up out of the blue and exposing her.

She still couldn't believe he'd tracked her down. No. She wasn't foolish enough to believe he'd taken the time and the trouble to find her out any sense of love or guilt. With Jared, it was about control. Possession. Evidently, he'd decided he missed that aspect of their relationship.

She didn't.

But she did miss what she'd just lost.

So much for happily-ever-after, she thought, as Mac

pulled into his garage and without a word and started unloading baby gifts.

So much for things finally being easy.

Three weeks passed in numbing, miserable silence. Shallie felt Mac pull farther and farther away from her. Farther and farther into himself.

He didn't act angry. If he had, maybe she could have handled it better. Instead, he acted indifferent. She was more than familiar with indifference. It's the best that she'd ever gotten from her mother. Indifference meant there would be no hitting, true, but the pain that lack of caring implied had almost been worse than a physical blow when she was a child. And the effect hung around much longer than a bruise.

It hurt as badly now.

So many times she wanted to ask him to say something. Anything. Curse. Belittle her. Berate her. Anything but this tepid, polite apathy. Anything but a cool good-night as he went to bed in the guest room and shut the door behind him.

No hugs. No kisses. No chocolate. She missed the chocolate most of all because it had become such a symbol of his love for her.

They were now husband and wife in name only. But he did his duty, this disillusioned husband of hers. He did what he had promised to do. He took care of her. He didn't have it in him to do anything else.

"Do you need anything from the supermarket?"

"When's your next doctor's appointment? Do you need me to take you?"

"I'll be at SW. Call me if you need anything."

That was about the extent of their conversation these days.

And it was slowly killing her right along with their marriage.

Tonight, when he came home from SW, was just another night in a string of nights where their communication consisted of short, guilty looks. He looked tired and haunted when he said a quiet, "Good night," and walked right past her without ever meeting her eyes.

That's probably the part that got to her most. She missed those smiling eyes. Missed the mischief. Missed the fun.

She'd done that to him. And it was this night that she'd finally had enough of dealing with the fallout.

With her heart in her throat she walked to the guest bedroom door. Knocked.

A few seconds passed before it opened.

Mac stood there in his bare feet, his shirt unbuttoned and tugged out of his pants.

"I give up," she said, before he could ask her what she wanted and make her feel even more of a pariah than she already felt.

He looked at her then. She'd given him little choice. All she saw was fatigue. Maybe a hint of anger.

It was the first real emotion she'd seen since that fateful day in March—and it spurred a surprising arch of anger in her.

"I'm sorry," she said. "It's too little. I know. But what else can I say? What else can I do?"

His jaw clenched and he looked away.

"Yeah. That's right. Look away. I'm sorry about that, too. That you can't even stand to look at me."

He scrubbed a weary hand over his jaw. "Look. I'm tired, okay? And I don't see what good this is doing."

"No. Of course you don't see. Your idea of dealing with what I've done to screw up *your* life is to ignore it.

"I've waited, Mac," she said, her voice rising in accusation. "I've waited. I've given you room. Hoped that with time you might talk to me. Might be able to forgive me. A lot to ask, I know. And why should you? I can't forgive myself. At least, I haven't been able to. But you know what? That stops right here. Right now. Tonight."

She was shaking now as almost a month of tightly wrapped emotions uncoiled like a spring inside her. She pushed past him, walked to the bed. Sat down on the edge of the mattress and braced her palms on either side of her hips.

"I made a mistake, okay? It was a horrible mistake. It wasn't my first. It probably won't be my last, but you know what, Mac? That doesn't make me a horrible person. A horrible person wouldn't have beat herself up over this. A horrible person wouldn't have left Georgia to avoid one mistake compounding into another."

"You're not a horrible person," he said with a grim reluctance that told her he wasn't one hundred percent convinced of that.

"Then why are you treating me like I am?" she implored, hearing the heartache, the humiliation, the disappointment in her voice and knowing he heard it, too.

He met her eyes, looked away. Again. Shook his

head. Again. "I don't know. Honest to God, Shallie. I don't know."

"I think you do," she said reacting to something she saw in that brief glimpse of his eyes. "I think you know exactly why. You just don't want to come to terms with it."

"Well. If you've got all the answers, by all means, enlighten me, then, will you?" There was just enough bite in his tone to let her know that the anger he'd bottled up all this time was near the bursting point.

Good. Because she was right there with him.

"I think the problem is that I'm not the same needy little girl who left here ten years ago. And you wanted me to be. You wanted me to be needy and perfect and a victim—just like I was back then."

"You let me think you were," he accused.

"Yeah," she said quietly. "Yeah. I did. I did because intuitively, I knew that's what you wanted me to be. I didn't want to let you down, Mac. From that first day we met when you were waiting for me on the school steps, I made it my mission to never let you down.

"And now I have," she said with her chin up. "And you reacted exactly the way I was always afraid you would. You turned away. You tuned me out."

"You lied to me," he said, a wealth of pain and defense in those four little words. "The last thing I expected from you was deceit."

"You think I don't know that? You think that wasn't a huge part of what stopped me from telling you the truth about the baby? I didn't want to disappoint you. You, the one person who always loved me.

"And now—" she lifted a hand, let it drop "—now I

have this chance for you to love not only me but my baby, too. Do you know what that means to me to know that my baby would actually have a father? A father like I never had? To have the *family* I never had?"

She felt tears push. She pushed back, determined not to give in to them now. "Did I lie? Yes. Was it wrong? Of course it was. Did I use you? Yes again. But I did something else, too, Mac. I loved you. There was nothing dishonest about that. It's all I had to give. It's all I've *ever* had to give anyone. And until you, it had never been enough."

She paused, met his eyes. "And you wonder why I lied? I lied because I was afraid of exactly what happened. I lied because I was afraid that like everyone else, my love wouldn't be enough for you, either. Turns out I had more than enough reason to be afraid."

When he said nothing, she knew it was over. She stood slowly, walked past him to the bedroom door. "Look…I got a response to the résumés I sent out a couple of weeks ago."

She stopped just inside the room, still hoping he'd say something, knowing in her heart that he wouldn't. "Actually got a job offer. So here's the deal. You won't have to worry about taking care of me anymore. But I would like a little time. A couple of weeks to find an apartment if that's okay. Then I'll be out of your hair."

She didn't expect him to follow her. And he didn't.

She walked to the bedroom they used to share, undressed in the dark and crawled under the covers. Tried not to remember the loving and the laughing they'd shared in this bed. Tried to reprogram, regroup and gear up for the next hurdle. Because that's what life was really all about. And that's what she always did to get by.

She'd be okay. She and her baby. They'd be fine. Just the two of them together.

Because that was the way it was going to be.

But she'd always be sorry. Always and forever be sorry that her love was never enough.

Eleven

Mac watched Shallie walk out the bedroom door. He had a lump in his throat the size of a football. Big enough anyway, that he blamed it for his silence.

Big enough that he blamed it for the burning going on behind his eyelids.

Feeling weary to the bone and as hollow as an empty well, he dragged his fingers through his hair. Flopped down on his back on the bed and stared at the ceiling.

What a mess. What a big, screwed-up mess.

Shallie's words kept replaying in his head, along with a litany of her sins.

He checked them off one by one, just as he'd been doing for days, rewinding and replaying and using them to distance himself from her emotionally.

She'd lied. She'd used. She'd deceived.

She'd slept with a married man.

Of all the transgressions he'd stacked up against her, the last one was the one that had been hanging him up the most. She'd committed adultery—just like his mother.

Yeah. He'd slogged around, knee-deep in those sins she'd committed against him for weeks now. Letting them build. Let them breed one on top of the other until he couldn't even look at her because that's all he saw. A liar. A cheater. A user.

But he had some new words to think about now. Words she'd delivered like a promise. A promise he knew she would keep.

Give me a couple of weeks. Then I'll be out of your hair.

Out of your hair...out of your hair...out of—

He sat up straight. Felt the kick of his heart. Felt the flood of panic spread through his chest.

She was leaving. She was letting him off the hook.

So, what did you think would happen, Einstein? Did you think she'd just hang around, like the ball and chain you'd decided she would always be? Just wear you down with the weight of her sins?

Out of your hair...out of your hair...

He swore into the darkness.

She'd do it, too. She'd leave him. For his sake. Because that was her true nature.

It all became so clear then. The accusation wheels stopped spinning in endless circles. What he hadn't been able to sort out in damn near a month slipped into place with the ease of the right combination on a safe lock.

All because her words made him realize what he'd be losing if he let her walk out that door.

God, he was a fool. The worst kind. The kind who couldn't see the beauty of a wildflower because his book of rules labeled it a noxious weed.

He rose, walked to the bedroom door. He had to fix this. He had to fix everything.

But it wouldn't be tonight, he realized when he carefully opened his master bedroom door and found her sleeping.

"Make it good," he told himself, and pulled on his shoes and socks. "Make it damn good."

And with that mission in mind, he slipped out of the house and started laying the groundwork for undoing the harm he'd done.

It was late the next morning when Shallie slipped out of the bedroom and ventured toward the kitchen. She hadn't slept well. She felt as rested as if she'd spent the night standing up in a corner—like a bad girl should, she thought morosely as she walked into the kitchen.

And stopped dead in her tracks.

Chocolate. There was chocolate everywhere.

Éclairs. Cake. Cookies. Candy. Tiramisu. Boxes and cartons and plates and trays of chocolate desserts of every size and description covered every inch of available counter space, some of it stacked layers deep.

"Thought you might have missed this, too."

Mac's voice startled her. She turned to see him standing just inside the kitchen, his fingers tucked in his back pockets, his hair a mess, his eyes blurry, as if he hadn't slept all night.

"I, um," She lifted a hand toward the mountains of chocolate. "I don't…understand."

But she hoped she did. She hoped with all her heart that the guilt she read in his eyes, the fact that he was looking at her, that he'd evidently bought the entire city of Bozeman out of chocolate by ten o'clock in the morning, meant that she understood perfectly what it meant.

Hope, it seemed, was stronger than despair. Because all he had to do was take a step toward her, hold out his hand and she was in his arms.

Clinging. Crying. Thanking God and her lucky stars and anything she could think of that she was in his arms again.

"I'm so sorry," he murmured into her hair. "So sorry for shutting you out."

"It's okay. It's okay," she whispered, beyond caring about how badly she'd hurt the past three weeks, only caring that he'd forgiven her.

"It's not okay," he said rocking her back and forth, holding her tight. "It's not okay at all.

"Come on," he said with a gentle squeeze. "Let's go into the living room. There are things I need to say to you."

She sniffed as, with his arm over her shoulders, he walked her to the sofa and sat her down.

"Nobody's perfect," he said, taking her hands in his and meeting her eyes. "And you were right. I wanted you to be. I expected you to be. And it wasn't until you pointed it out that I realized what a jerk I was."

"You weren't a jerk. I hurt you."

He shook his head. "I was a jerk," he restated emphatically. "Hell, Shall—I was a *perfect* jerk. Perfect life. Perfect business. Perfect woman for me to take care of and play perfect husband for."

He made a face that told of his self-disgust. "That's what happens when Peter Pan grows up to be a man. He expects the status quo. And he can't handle it when something happens that doesn't fit his standard, so he cuts it out of his life."

He wanted to talk, so she let him. Knew, instinctively that he was working his way through his thoughts very carefully.

"Well, life's not perfect. And you know what happens to a man who expects perfection? He loses out on some of the best things in his life." His gaze dropped to their joined hands before meeting her eyes again. "I don't want to lose you, Shallie. I don't want to lose what we had. I don't want to lose the most important thing that ever happened to me. Don't go. Please don't go."

Well, damn. She was crying again. "I'm not going anywhere," she managed to whisper between the tears. "You're stuck with me, Mac. You just try and shake me loose. See what happens."

"I love you, Shallie. I love you so much."

She wrapped herself around him. Held him close. "That's enough for me. That will always be enough."

And for the first time in her life she knew that what she had to offer—her love—was finally enough, too.

Epilogue

Ella Margaret McDonald came screaming and kicking into the world at 3:26 a.m. on June 9.

"Just like her momma," Mac whispered as he snuggled his baby daughter in his arms three hours later while Shallie dozed in her hospital bed.

"She's beautiful, Mac," his mother said with tears in her eyes and with a love he had missed for too many years.

Yeah, Mr. Perfect had learned a lot from his scrapper of a wife. He'd learned to forgive. And he'd learned that picking up the phone and calling his mother wasn't such a hard thing to do after all. In fact, next to marrying Shallie, it was one of the easiest and the best things he'd ever done.

Hearing the joy in his mother's voice when she'd realized he was letting her back in his life again took some of the bite out of the guilt he felt over turning away from her.

He'd told his dad first, of course. Told him that it was time for both of them to get on with life and learn to live with the truth of it. Yeah, it had hurt his dad at first, but he was a fair man. Of course, the fact that Widow Hammel had started making him pot roast on Sundays and keeping him company a couple of nights a week also helped.

"Hi, sleepyhead," Mac murmured when Shallie opened her eyes and blinked up at him.

"Hey. How's our girl?"

"Little Gertrude is doing just fine," he teased, knowing he'd get a grin out of her. "How's her momma?"

"Good," she said, shifting gingerly. "I'm good."

Mac leaned down and kissed her. "You're better than good, short-stack. In my book, you're *almost* perfect."

And that, Mac knew, was the best anyone could ever hope to be.

* * * * *

THE BODYGUARDS
The thrilling series continues.
OVER THE LINE—June 2006
UNDER THE WIRE—Winter 2006/2007
from Cindy Gerard and St. Martin's Press.

Silhouette BOMBSHELL™

The Marian priestesses were destroyed long ago, but their daughters live on. The time has come for the heiresses to learn of their legacy, to unite the pieces of a powerful mosaic and bring light to a secret their ancestors died to protect.

The Madonna Key

Follow their quests each month.

Lost Calling by Evelyn Vaughn,
July 2006

Haunted Echoes by Cindy Dees,
August 2006

Dark Revelations by Lorna Tedder,
September 2006

Shadow Lines by Carol Stephenson,
October 2006

Hidden Sanctuary by Sharron McClellan,
November 2006

Veiled Legacy by Jenna Mills,
December 2006

Seventh Key by Evelyn Vaughn,
January 2007

**Hidden in the secrets of antiquity,
lies the unimagined truth...**

Introducing

ROGUE Angel™

a brand-new line filled with mystery
and suspense, action and adventure,
and a fascinating look into history.
And it all begins with DESTINY.

In a sealed crypt in
France, where the
terrifying legend of
the beast of Gevaudan
begins to unravel,
Annja Creed discovers
a stunning artifact
that will seal her destiny.

*Available every other
month starting
July 2006, wherever
you buy books.*

Hidden in the secrets
of antiquity, lies the
unimagined truth...

ROGUE Angel
Alex Archer
DESTINY

GOLD EAGLE #2119
$6.50 U.S. $7.99 CAN.

GRA1

If you enjoyed what you just read,
then we've got an offer you can't resist!

Take 2 bestselling
love stories FREE!
Plus get a FREE surprise gift!

Clip this page and mail it to Silhouette Reader Service™

IN U.S.A.	IN CANADA
3010 Walden Ave.	P.O. Box 609
P.O. Box 1867	Fort Erie, Ontario
Buffalo, N.Y. 14240-1867	L2A 5X3

YES! Please send me 2 free Silhouette Desire® novels and my free surprise gift. After receiving them, if I don't wish to receive anymore, I can return the shipping statement marked cancel. If I don't cancel, I will receive 6 brand-new novels every month, before they're available in stores! In the U.S.A., bill me at the bargain price of $3.80 plus 25¢ shipping and handling per book and applicable sales tax, if any*. In Canada, bill me at the bargain price of $4.47 plus 25¢ shipping and handling per book and applicable taxes**. That's the complete price and a savings of at least 10% off the cover prices—what a great deal! I understand that accepting the 2 free books and gift places me under no obligation ever to buy any books. I can always return a shipment and cancel at any time. Even if I never buy another book from Silhouette, the 2 free books and gift are mine to keep forever.

225 SDN DZ9F
326 SDN DZ9G

Name	(PLEASE PRINT)	
Address	Apt.#	
City	State/Prov.	Zip/Postal Code

Not valid to current Silhouette Desire® subscribers.

Want to try two free books from another series?
Call 1-800-873-8635 or visit www.morefreebooks.com.

* Terms and prices subject to change without notice. Sales tax applicable in N.Y.
** Canadian residents will be charged applicable provincial taxes and GST.
  All orders subject to approval. Offer limited to one per household.
  ® are registered trademarks owned and used by the trademark owner and or its licensee.

DES04R   ©2004 Harlequin Enterprises Limited

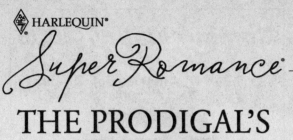

HARLEQUIN®

Super Romance

THE PRODIGAL'S RETURN

by Anna DeStefano

Prom night for Jenn Gardner and Neal Cain turned
into a tragedy that tore them apart. Eight years
later, Jenn has made a life for herself and her young
daughter. But when Neal comes home, Jenn sees that
he is still consumed with the past. Maybe she can
convince him that he's paid enough and deserves
happiness a second time around.

"Anna DeStefano's remarkable stories of the healing
power of love touch the heart with hope. One of the
genre's rising stars..."
—Gayle Wilson, two-time
RITA® Award-winning author

On sale July 2006!
*Available wherever books are sold, including most
bookstores, supermarkets, discount stores and drugstores.*

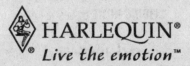

HARLEQUIN®
Live the emotion™

COMING NEXT MONTH

#1735 UNDER DEEPEST COVER—Kara Lennox
The Elliotts
He needed her help, she needed his protection, but posing as lovers could prove to be risky…and every bit the scandal.

**#1736 THE TEXAN'S CONVENIENT MARRIAGE—
Peggy Moreland**
A Piece of Texas
A Texan's plans to keep his merger of convenience casual are ruined when passion enters the marriage bed.

#1737 THE ONE-WEEK WIFE—Patricia Kay
Secret Lives of Society Wives
A fake honeymoon turns into an ardent escapade when the wedding planner plays the millionaire's wife for a week.

**#1738 EXPOSING THE EXECUTIVE'S SECRETS—
Emilie Rose**
Trust Fund Affairs
Buying her ex at a charity bachelor auction seemed the perfect way to settle the score, until the sparks start flying again.

**#1739 THE MILLIONAIRE'S PREGNANT MISTRESS—
Michelle Celmer**
Rich and Reclusive
A stolen night of passion. An unplanned pregnancy. Was a forced marriage next?

#1740 TO CLAIM HIS OWN—Mary Lynn Baxter
He'd returned to claim his child—but his son's beautiful guardian was not giving up without a fight.

SDCNM0606